GHOST HUNTRESS

THE JOURNEY

GHOST HUNTRESS

THE JOURNEY

BOOK 6

MARLEY GIBSON

Copyright Information

eISBN: 978-1-937776-43-5
ISBN: 978-1-937776-74-9

Praise for the Ghost Huntress Series

"This book has suspense, chills, and adventure—everything ghost hunting should be!"

~ Zak Bagans, star of Travel Channel's *Ghost Adventures*

"Every young woman needs to read this!"

~ Steve Gonzalves, of SyFy Channel's *Ghost Hunters* and *Ghost Hunters Academy*

"Real life ghost huntress, Marley Gibson, pulls no punches."

~ Jason Hawes and Grant Wilson, stars of SyFy Channel's *Ghost Hunters*

"Kendall's witty narrative voice (she quotes Shakespeare and Ugly Betty with equal aplomb) drives this fast-paced, wholesome-with-an-edge tale.

~ *Publishers Weekly Review*

"This book reads like a good episode of your favorite ghost-hunting show.... Teens who watch Ghost Whisperer or Haunting Evidence... will eat this up...."

~*Booklist*

v

"*Ghost Huntress* has it all - mystery, romance, ghost hunting and a quirky psychic teen named Kendall who I'd love to be friends with!"

~ Simone Elkeles, *New York Times* bestselling author

"Marley Gibson's heroine, Kendall, walks into the room and the party starts. She's your ebullient friend from high school, always ready with a joke, who can't be kept down and won't let you stay down, either."

~ Jenn Echols, award-winning author, MTV Books

READ THESE OTHER BOOKS BY MARLEY GIBSON

Ghost Huntress Series - Young Adult/Paranormal

Ghost Huntress: The Awakening
Ghost Huntress: The Guidance
Ghost Huntress: The Reason
Ghost Huntress: The Counseling
Ghost Huntress: The Discovery
Ghost Huntress: The Journey
Ghost Huntress: The Tidings, A Christmas Novella

Other Young Adult Books

Radiate

Non-Fiction

The Other Side: A Teen's Guide to Ghost
Hunting and the Paranormal
with Patrick Burns

New Adult Books

Poser

Books for Adults

Can't Touch This (Resisting Temptation series)
Can't Fight This (Resisting Temptation series)

"Let your mind start a journey through a strange new world. Leave all thoughts of the world you knew before. Let your soul take you where you long to be. Close your eyes and let your spirit soar and you'll live as you've never lived before."

— Erich Fromm

CHAPTER ONE

I can't believe I'm on my way to freakin' Europe for a month! And I'm flying first class, at that.

Whodathunkit? Certainly not me. But thanks to a surprise trust fund that fell into my lap from my birth family, I'm able to join the famous TV psychic Oliver Bates, and other enlightened teens, on a jaunt through Europe, ghost hunting, investigating, and connecting with a whole new crop of spirits.

This has been the whirl-windy tsunami hurricane of an existence if I've ever known one. My dad's job moved us from Chicago to Radisson, Georgia, where I started having my psychic awakening. Through all of that, I've had to deal with a school bully, a new boyfriend coming into my life, then moving to Alaska, forming a ghost hunting team with my new friends, having a near death experience, and finding out that I'm adopted and both of my parents are deceased. All of this is enough to put any normal person on a good cocktail of medications. Me, I take it in stride and just blink hard at the challenges I continue to face.

Fortunately, this leg of my life journey seems to be a little less challenging at the moment.

I squiggle down into the comfort of my airline seat and let out a contented sigh. These British Airways sleep pods are completely the bomb. Okay, so maybe people don't use that phrase anymore, but it's the best way to describe the personal cocoon I have here to myself as we wing over the ocean to our destination. Then again, maybe one shouldn't use the word "bomb" when on an international flight. Bad Kendall!

My birth dad's twin sister, Andi Caminiti Norwich (my chaper-one for the summer thanks to an agreement with my parents), is sacked out behind me in her own personal pod. She's wearing the complimentary eye mask, jammies, and is snoring slightly. Good thing I can put my ear buds in if she gets more boisterous. It's been amazing having Aunt Andi in my life and getting to know her and hear stories about my real dad.

Don't get me wrong, I still greatly consider the Mooreheads my *real* parents since, like, they chose to adopt me and raise me as their own. They still take excellent care of me and provide for me. There is, though, that itch to complete the full circle to connect with my birth family. My former spirit guide, Emily, turned out to be my mom, and then faded away. I haven't been able to connect with my dad, but I do have a lead on Emily's parents possibly living in Italy.

Which brings me to another reason I'm on this overseas jaunt.

I glance over to the pod right next to me where my best friend, Celia Nichols, has made camp. She's playing some science experi-ment building game on her tablet computer where it looks like she's blowing things up. I wonder sometimes if she shouldn't have been born male. She's such a thirteen year old boy at times. She's bobbing her head in time to music flowing from her headphones, her dark hair softly swinging. Celia's (gladly!) tagging along this summer to help out with whatever paranormal investigations we run across in our travels. Since she's all about being the rich girl in Radisson with the AmEx card, it was easy for her to cash in points and join me here in first class.

She was pouty right after we took off from Atlanta for our over-night flight to London. Before our dinner arrived and the first movie started—a classic showing of *Chitty Chitty Bang Bang...* who knew James Bond's Ian Fleming wrote that?!—I managed to get out of her that she and Clay Price, her boyfriend, had decided to "take the summer off." Although Celia's a glamazon in her own right and doesn't even know it, I can tell this turn of events has bummed her out to no end. Clay was the first guy she ever dated. The first and only one she ever kissed.

Well, the heck with him and his loss. Been there, done that. Have the T-shirt.

I'm glad she's getting out to spread her wings in the Old World. Rather, a new world to us.

Another sigh escapes me. This time, it's one of disappointment. My sweetie, Patrick Lynn, isn't on the flight with us. Don't get me wrong, he's going to Europe. However, to save some money—i.e. to spend it overseas instead—Patrick opted to fly stand-by on a military flight since his father is active Air Force. He actually got called out to Dobbins Air Force Base last night to get on a transport plane and should be waiting for me at Heathrow when we land in the UK tomorrow.

Patrick and I've been together since we met in California at Oliver Bates's enlightened kids camp. We're so much the same person, what with both of us being psychic and being so connected to each other. He's perfect for me and I'm crazy about him. We just haven't said the "L" word to each other... yet.

I stop flipping through the channels on my television and sit back. It's going to be amazing to work with Oliver Bates again, as well as other psychic teens, in investigating the paranormal in Europe. I'm so glad my mom and dad let me do this and I know I'll make memories to last a lifetime. It's also a chance to bond with Aunt Andi and maybe follow up on the visions I've had of my *real* mother, Emily's, parents in Italy. Of course, Italy's our last stop on this journey. First things first in London, then off to Paris where another member of our ghost huntress team, Becca Asiaf, is competing in the DanceFest for DJs festival. She's the best DJ I've ever watched and listened to, so I know she's going to blow them away in Europe.

"Kendall, you want me to give you a facial?" Taylor Tillson asks from the row in front of me. Her long tresses are pulled away from her face with a cloth skull headband and her beautiful face is slathered in some sort of conditioning cream. Taylor's the photographer for our ghost huntress team. She just returned to Radisson from a short stint in Alaska where she had to go live with her father when her mother had to go into a rehab hospital.

I smile, so happy to see her face again on a regular basis. "A what?" I ask with a giggle.

She lifts her cosmetic bag full of under-three-ounce containers of every kind of skin care product on the planet. "I saw this YouTube video on how British business woman use overseas travel to give themselves sort of a spa treatment. I thought it looked *tres chic*, so *voila!*"

Oh boy, Taylor's going to be unbearably French when we hit Paris in a couple of weeks. It's totally her thing.

"Thanks, Tay-Tay. I think I'll pass for now."

She holds up three bottles of glittery nail polish. "A mani then?"

I screw up my nose thinking of the diffusion and how the pungent smell would soon fill the first class cabin. My nails are too short anyway from biting them all the time thanks to whatever random ghost, entity, or spirit guide appears to me. "No thanks, Tay. I think I'll just chill the rest of the way."

She waves me off with a wink and a smile and returns to her spa set up.

A snicker across the aisle pulls at my ear.

"The girl needs professional help," a deep voice says.

Yeah...that's right. Taylor's twin brother, my ex, Jason Tillson sits ten feet away from me. Way too close for comfort.

"Considering what your mom just went through, I don't think that's a funny joke, Jason," I say firmly. I've touched a raw nerve with him.

"Whatever," he says and then looks back at his sister. "She's making a mess."

"She's having fun," I snip back without making eye contact with the blue eyes that I know for a fact are scrutinizing my every move. "Let her be."

Jason laughs softly again. "Have you just met me?"

His quip is meant to be amusing, but it's anything but. No... I've known Jason for almost a year. In which time, we've gone from fussing at each other, to falling for each other, to making out with each other, to saying we *loved* each other, to him up and leaving

4

town to move to Alaska and hook up with some skank named Zelda. Oh, did I go there? You bet I did.

I'm so not happy that Jason is on this trip. He doesn't believe in the paranormal and is only here to keep a watchful eye on his sister… and me. Their mother recently returned to work for her airline and was able to get the Tillson twins good discounts for their European spree. I couldn't be happier that Taylor got to come with us. I'm *not* so thrilled that Jason is here.

He's … too close. Europe's a big continent, yet something tells me it's going to get a heck of a lot smaller with the two of us in such close proximity.

The flight attendant removes my dinner tray that I came close to licking clean. Filet mignon, roasted potatoes, and grilled asparagus. Who said airplane food was nasty? I'm drinking Sprite Zero and pretending it's expensive French champagne. Mmm…

I lift my eyes and glance over at Jason. His black shirt is stretched across his chest and I see his long, bare toes poking out from the end of his jeans that are covered by the airplane blanket. He tosses a way-too-charming smile my way and I glower in his general direction. Celia clicks her tongue as if to tell me to behave.

"He hasn't done anything," she whispers to me.

"Not yet," I mutter back.

I've totally avoided Jason since he showed up at my house for the post-prom brunch my mom and I hosted. It was, like, so inappropriate of him to just come barging into the house while we were all still celebrating and paired off. Patrick had sensed it then, too, and had clasped my hand for support. Or to mark his territory. One or the other. Talk about an awkward moment! I've never wanted a sink hole to open up underneath me so much in my life. Some psychic I am, huh? Didn't see *that* coming!

Celia moves from her pod over to mine. I scoot over to make room for her five miles of legs. "I just got an e-mail from Oliver with our London itinerary," she tells me.

I take her tablet computer and scroll through the many things Oliver has in store for us. Interviews with the media, tours of famous

British places, an investigation at a castle or two, and— "What's this one?" I point to an item on the list.

However, Celia isn't listening. She's watching. Not me. Jason Tillson.

I follow her gaze and then blink hard, understanding just why she's gawking his way.

Across the aisle, Jason has tugged off his black t-shirt to expose his finely tanned rib cage and muscular back. What the...

I see Celia gulp noticeably. Who can blame her? The guy is a work of art.

Thankfully, he tugs on the British Airways t-shirt that came free in our pods as sleep clothes.

I nudge Celia with my elbow and giggle. "Down girl."

She pops to attention. "What? Huh? Oh, I just thought I saw—"

"A hot guy. I know. Get over it."

Celia's cheeks heat, but she shakes her head. "Whatever, Kendall. It's just weird to have him along. I mean, Taylor's going to take pics, and I'm here to draw any spirit experiences you have. There's not really any reason for Jason to be here."

"Other than being over-protective of Taylor, and to tell the rest of us what we can and can't do," I say.

She steals one last glance at the guy she's known her whole life. "I just think he's going to be bored this summer."

I shrug. "Not my boyfriend... not my problem." Handing Celia back her tablet, I say, "You know, let's just deal with the schedule when we get there. We've got a long flight. You should relax and crawl into your pod. Play with all the buttons and stuff, surf the web, watch a movie."

Celia smiles at me and shakes her head. "You don't fool me, Kendall. I know you've still got feelings for him."

I stop clicking through my movie channels and give my bestie an incredulous look. "Umm, no, I don't. I just don't want him ruining this trip in any way, shape, form, or fashion."

Celia returns to her pod where she nabs her change of clothes and her toothbrush. She turns before heading to the bathroom.

"Keep telling yourself that, Kendall. 'The course of true love never did run smooth,'" she says in a fake British accent.

I roll my eyes at her Shakespearean reference to *A Midsummer Night's Dream* and want one of my own. "Good night, William."

Celia walks off toward the bathroom and I hunker down into my pod. I cue up the Audrey Hepburn/Humphrey Bogart/William Holden version of *Sabrina* and try not to think about the love triangle plot in the movie and how it mirrors my own existence.

My psychic senses tell me this summer is going to be anything but boring.

CHAPTER TWO

Before I even lift my eyelids, I know I'm being watched.
Like the proverbial hawk.

When I do finally peek, I see no feathers. Only blazing blue eyes that are more incredible and deeper than I remember. Jason's perched on the edge of his pod with his tanned arms crossed over the top and his chin resting on them. A skittle of electricity jolts through me at the sight of him gazing at me and I find myself sucking in a treacherous gasp.

I hate myself.

"Kendall, we need to talk," he says, breaking the silence in first class cabin.

In order to avoid more traitorous reactions from my body, I pull the sleep blanket up over my head to hide my face and block out the image of Jason Tillson all fresh from sleep.

He laughs at me, a deep mirth that starts low in his stomach and bubbles up and out. "You're just as adorable as ever."

Rage boils under my skin, bringing me fully awake. He's not allowed to talk to me like this. No matter what. We broke up. He left. I moved on. I'm with someone else.

"I'm serious, Kendall," he adds.

That does it. I swiftly toss the blanket off me and say, "As adorable as Zelda?"

Ooo... I went there.

Zelda's the skank he apparently hooked up with while he lived in Alaska with his dad. I didn't need his sister, Taylor, to report this fact to me because Jason's Facebook page had plenty of Instagram pictures of the two of them together rock climbing, salmon fishing, and other outdoorsy activities.

Jason's eyes widen with nothing short of shock. He opens his mouth to speak, but thinks better than to do so.

At just that moment, Hyacinth, the flight attendant who's been taking care of us, appears in the aisle. "Good morning, miss. Are you ready for breakfast?"

I sit up tall at the thought of more free food. Anything to distract me from Jason's intrusion. "Sure. Whatcha got?"

"Full English fry-up," she says with a smile. "Fried eggs, bacon, sausages, fried bread, baked beans, and mushrooms. I'll set you right up."

Inwardly, I cringe at the thought of what such a meal will do to my young arteries. However, I give Hyacinth a big smile and nod.

She turns to Jason. "I'll bring you a tray, too, love."

Love? Hardly.

I stop myself, halting the flow of angry lava through my veins. I swallow my pride and then say to Jason, "You know, you don't owe me any explanation. It is what it is."

"No, it was what it was, Kendall. The future can be anything we want it to be."

"Maybe, but my *present* is with Patrick," I say firmly.

"Oh, him." Jason groans and tosses his arms up, nearly knocking the tray of steaming, hot teacups out of Hyacinth's hands.

"Careful, love," she says with a smile. "Here you go. Your breakfast will be out straight away."

I take the mug of steeping tea and blow on the top. Anything not to look at Jason or be pulled into the depths of trouble those blue eyes offer. Jason and I had our brief time together and I'll always cherish it. I'm with Patrick now. The guy with the deep-chocolate eyes, the sexy singing voice, and the psychic connection through our minds. I wonder if he can hear me this far away.

Patrick? Are you there?

"Kendall..." Jason presses.

I don't look his way. I sense the frown on my face when Patrick doesn't respond to me psychically. I suppose an ocean between us has something to do with it.

Jason won't leave me the hell alone, though… turning up like a bad habit every time I lift my eyes. Is this what it's going to be like all summer? I don't know if I have the strength to fight him off. And what's the deal with my heartbeat getting all freaky and double-pounding when he says my name and the mere sight of him all mussed and stubbled from sleeping on the airplane.

"Kendall," he says a bit louder this time.

"Here we go, love," Hyacinth says, setting a lovely tray of food in front of me. Typically, I wouldn't go for baked beans as a breakfast food, but when in Rome… err… London.

"Come on, Kendall," Jason stresses.

I pop up and raise my eyebrows. "I'm eating here, hello!"

He turns as I dive into my meal. Nothing like yummy food to distract me from the cute guy who won't leave me alone.

✢ ✢ ✢

The Kendall has landed! And I'm in the motherland.

Okay, so my adopted surname, Moorehead, is Scottish. Still, it's part of the British Isles. And I couldn't be happier to be here.

Celia bounces in place in front of me in line at Customs as she hoists up her backpack onto her shoulder. Taylor, perfectly coifed and makeup'd from her overseas beauty treatment, smiles from ear to ear, frantically checking her Twitter and Tumblr accounts.

"This is so exciting!" she says with a bit of a squee in her voice. "I'm going to Tweet non-stop all summer and do an amazing photo blog."

"Do you think we'll be able to go to Stratford-Upon-Avon to see Shakespeare's birthplace?" Celia asks.

Jason nudges her. "You have an obsession with The Bard, huh? Always have, since like third grade."

Celia's cheeks splash bright fuchsia at his words, and I can see with my mind's eye that the childhood crush Celia once had on

Jason Tillson is still simmering beneath the surface. It's weird to think that these guys have known each other their whole lives, yet I've only been part of the group for under a year.

Taylor interjects, "If we can't take a day trip out of the city, Celia, we can always go to the Globe Theatre in London. Maybe even catch a show."

"That would be cool," Celia says as she tucks her black hair behind her ears. I think of that One Direction song, *You Don't Know You're Beautiful*, when I think of Celia. She's tall and thin and has such a naturally pretty face hidden behind her dark hair. She was really coming into her own... until stupid Clay Price broke up with her. What a jerk. Why didn't I see that coming? You'd think with my psychic abilities, I could give my friends more of head's up when things are headed their way. Of course, maybe that's not how it works. No lottery numbers for me or easy answers on tests, but in terms of connecting with lost spirits, I'm your girl.

Speaking of, there's an oddly-placed gentleman standing in front of us in the passport line. His clothing of thick wool and jacket trimmed in fur—in the dead of summer—tells me that he's no tourist on a cheap vacation package to enjoy the exchange rate of the dollar versus the euro. He's... from the past. Leather pants and thick boots make me think he's from the World War II era.

"Excuse me, miss. Perhaps I can assist you," he says to me. "May I show you around?"

I freeze up, unsure at first if maybe I'm wrong and he's some sort of costumed entertainment at Heathrow airport, not a real apparition addressing me directly. He looks pretty authentic in his leather and with those goggles around his neck. Almost too good. He's got to be an actor. Right?

I shift my eyes over to Celia to get a reality check. "Do you see him?"

She glances about. "Which him? There are, like, three hundred people in line."

"The World War II pilot standing to my left."

The pilot shakes his head at me. "Oh my, this isn't working."

11

"What isn't?" I ask him.

The ghost stares at me. "I'll have to try something else."

Then he fades away.

Celia grins at me. "Oh, it's started already! Excellent." She sets her backpack down and reaches for her sketch pad. "Tell me all about him and I'll draw him for you. You know Heathrow Airport was constructed from land from the former Heath Row farmers market area, hence the name. It was first established in 1929 as a small aircraft field and then in 1944, the land was used primarily for military aircraft, so that more than likely explains the—"

I stop her with my hands. "Never mind. He's gone."

Taylor nudges me from behind before I can overthink the brief close encounter. "Your turn, Kendall."

I step up to the counter where the worker barely glances up at me. He seems exhausted, even at this early morning hour, from dealing with some many incoming flights to his country. He takes my passport and scans it through some machine before flipping through the empty pages. This may be my first time out of America, but I know it won't be my last.

"Purpose of your visit?"

Technically it's business, but I don't say that. "Summer vacation."

"How long will you be in the United Kingdom?"

"Two weeks," I say, feeling like I'm taking a college entry exam.

He still hasn't glanced up at me. "What's your occupation?"

I try not to laugh. "Umm, I'm in high school."

Finally, he lifts his head, realizing he doesn't have to go through the stiff business routine anymore, and smiles at me. A crooked-toothed grin, but a grin nonetheless. Then he punches a stamp into my passport and slides it back to me. "Welcome to the United Kingdom, dearie. Enjoy your stay."

I retrieve my documents and pass through. I'm on British soil now, officially! So much to look forward to this summer... yet. There it is. The wave of nausea. The searing pain. Suddenly, the psychic headache begins to tap at my skull on the left side. Hard. Menacing, almost. Dread overwhelms me, starting at the tips of my toes and flaming out the top of my head. I'm cold and scared and locked in place. Not freaked out that I'm in a foreign country without my parents or anything. It's more like there's a niggling in my head telling me something's not... *right.*

I turn and watch passengers from other planes slip through the bonds of the customs check out. Waves of psychic energy reverberate from all of them. The man in the turban is worried about how much a cab into London will cost. The small Asian woman fears she won't make it to the Royal London Hospital in time to see her dying sister. The French couple holding hands and making out are afraid...*ooo!*...they're having an affair and are afraid their spouses will find out. So not my business! But, hey... some advice? Don't mack on each other in a public place where everyone has a cell phone with a camera and video recorder. Duh!

But this is no laughing matter. There are others. Spirits. Entities hanging around the living. Random ghosts from centuries gone by. Not just a few hundred years of existence, like my own homeland. Rather, England has the psychic energy of *thousands* of years hanging onto the shorelines, the cliffs, the cities, and the countryside. It's like a blasting wave of electricity reaching out to me, warning me, almost. A peasant woman stands in one corner, wandering, lost. A Beefeater stands guard—of what?—a few feet away. A dirty ragamuffin of a kid is chasing an equally grimy mutt. Something tells me none of these people are props or actors of any sort.

I rub my eyes and shake my head hard trying to catch my breath. Aunt Andi approaches from behind and rubs her hand across my shoulder.

"Kendall, is everything all right?"

I nod, but say, "No. Not really. Just getting long distant messages from ghosts of centuries past."

Andi's eyes shift to concern. "Loreen said this might happen. What with you still having your psychic awakening and spirits knowing they can come knock on your skull, so to speak."

I wince. "What do you mean?"

My aunt smiles. "These centuries-old ghosts see fresh meat. You basically have a neon sign over your head. You've got to shut yourself off the best you can."

Talk about the ultimate history assignment if I were to help Mary Queen of Scots find her chopped off head, or help the Jacobites with their uprising in the Battle of Culloden, or help Richard the Lionhearted pass into the light. Or even meet Shakespeare and ask him if he really wrote all those stories or if Christopher Marlowe did it. That would be the penultimate of coolness. That's not what I'm here for, though. I'm here to work with Oliver on his important cases. That's what I've got to focus on. We're here to help the living, not the dead.

"So what did Loreen say?"

"She said you have to protect yourself not only in a bubble of white light around you, but you have to make sure you visualize the light going through you, penetrating you, coming in and out and forming a fortress around you to keep these spirits at bay."

A spiritual suit of armor. Makes sense to me. "I'll make sure I protect myself, Aunt Andi. Thanks."

She smiles and touches her forehead to mine. "Just call me Andi, sweetie. I'm so happy to be with you on this trip."

I hug her to me. "I'm so happy to have you in my life."

"Hey, you're blocking the aisle!" Celia says kiddingly.

"And I happen to know there's a gorgeous guy waiting for you," Taylor says, holding up an iPhone that shows Patrick's recent Facebook post and then reads, "Waiting for Kendall at Heathrow Airport. I can feel her getting nearer…" She puts a hand to her heart. "That is the sweetest thing ever."

Thank heavens Jason has his ear buds in; otherwise I'm sure there's be some extensive color commentary.

Who cares, though! I can't wait to see my sweetie. He's here. I just have to find him.

I bob and weave through the rest of the terminal, making my way to the escalator that takes me to baggage claim. The terminal building is silver-shiny and very high-tech and modern looking.

You'd never know it was merely a crossroad for destinations and journeys.

And then I see him. Actually, I *feel* him first. A bright, spreading warmth coats me in love and comfort from the inside out. Patrick Lynn is here waiting for me. My feet carry me forward on the terminal floor, past the hordes of people waiting for their bags at the incoming Berlin flight.

At carousel number eight, I barely see our flight number from Atlanta displayed on the board. Instead, I spot the familiar head of brown hair and the gorgeous brown eyes peering out over a white cardboard sign that reads: *I *heart* Kendall Moorehead.*

Did Patrick just tell me he loves me?

"Awww... *c'est si romantique,*" Taylor says with her hand over her heart again.

I see Jason roll his eyes and then gag like an eleven-year-old boy, until Celia smacks him hard in the stomach and he stops.

"Hey, babe!" Patrick shouts out, obviously not hearing my psychically-posed inquiry. Oh well, I'll drop it for now. I'm just so damn happy to see him.

I run the last few steps toward him and literally throw myself into his arms. He lifts me off the floor and swings me about as though I weigh nothing at all. (Not an option after that fattening breakfast!) He sets me down and kisses me firmly on the lips. I totally want to make out with him more, but this isn't the place. Instead, I lace my fingers up into his thick hair and hug him again.

"I thought you'd never get here," Patrick says close to my ear. "This is so cool. We're going to have an amazing summer together."

Just as I relax into Patrick's arms, I see *him* again. The World War II pilot. He's off to the side of carousel five, and he looks so much like he wants to tell me something. I shake him off and close my eyes, building that white light reinforcement around me for protection.

When I open my eyes, he's gone.

I hope that's the last I see of him.

CHAPTER THREE

"I can't believe Tillson is here," Patrick mutters to me.

"Taylor's part of my team," I say as I watch the bags parade around the belt in front of us.

Patrick frowns at me. "You know I mean Jason."

"Ignore him, Patrick. That's what I plan on doing."

I want to believe that, Kendall.

I sigh. *I don't have feelings for him anymore.*

He has them for you, though.

That's his problem.

With that, I turn to Patrick. "Enough." Then I lean and point at my black suitcase. "That's it. That's the last one."

He hauls it up off the belt and lets out a giant-sized groan. "Holy crap, Kendall. What did you put in here? Kaitlyn?"

I giggle at the thought of my little sister stowing away in my bag. "No, fortunately the brat is at soccer camp in Florida. A long way from me. I just brought changes of clothes, bathing suits, dresses… shoes."

He shakes his head. "How many pair?"

"I don't know; I didn't count," I say firmly.

"Patrick, darling," Taylor says, nearing us, "a woman never needs to justify the amount of items—clothing, jewelry, or makeup—that she requires to be beautiful for her man."

"Kendall's perfect just as she is."

Taylor gives me the doe-eyed look for the fourth time in the last ten minutes. "Honestly, Kendall. He's a keeper."

I'm about to respond when I hear my name called out and see a red-headed blur coming at me.

"Jessica!" I shout out and run to meet her halfway. We meet in a tangled mess of gangly arms and legs hugging and squealing.

"Oh, my God! I can't believe we're in England!" she says exuberantly.

Jessica Spencer was my roommate at Oliver's enlightened kids' retreat in California. We've kept in touch via e-mail and social media, but haven't seen each other since. This is really awesome to be able to spend more time with a west coast friend and someone who's also dealing with paranormal phenomena in her own life.

"Have you seen the Pucketts?" she asks. Maddie, Erin, and Harper Puckett from Alabama were also at the retreat with us. We'd been told by Oliver that the girls were invited along on the trip.

"Did someone say my name?" I hear the high-pitched southern drawl say.

I spin around and see Maddie Puckett, without her sisters, in a bright yellow sundress and sunglasses perched atop her head of golden hair.

Hugs and air kisses are disbursed and Patrick moves in to hug the two girls as well. He takes their bags and adds them on to the rolling palate that already holds our own.

"Well, if it's not old home week," Maddie says with a wide grin. "Too bad Harper and Erin opted for cheerleader camp instead."

"Are they crazy?" Celia blurts out.

Maddie winks. "A little." Then she spots Jason. "And who are you?"

Taylor steps up. "He's my twin brother. Watch out for him."

Maddie smiles brightly. "I don't know if I want to." If southern charm actually oozed, we'd all be standing in a big old mess of it right about now.

Jason, being a southern gentleman himself, extends his hand. "Hey, I'm Jason." Then he drops contact and goes back to reading messages on his phone.

Maddie glances over at me. "Your ex?"

"Yep."

Her eyes shift over to Patrick. "And your current?"

"Yep."

She smiles wickedly. "Excellent."

A man in a blue uniform approaches our group. "I'm looking for Oliver Bates's group from America."

"That's us!" Celia says.

"Please follow me. I'm here to take you on a tour of the city, and then deliver you to your hotel accommodations."

Very posh.

We gather everything and head outside to the waiting area where a perfect, red double-decker bus is idling. There are people on the top deck, but I don't know who they are. I try to hone in with my psychic senses, but I'm not getting anything. It's like there's a shield there. A steel wall of sorts that I can't see through.

"This is wicked cool," Celia says and then climbs up onto the first level of the bus.

Taylor has pulled out her Nikon and is snapping pictures in burst mode. Patrick steps up into the bus and then reaches behind him and extends his hand to me. So sweet. I accept it and follow him onto our transport. The guy in the blue uniform is taking care of all of our bags, so I head to the back of the bus and slide up the tiny spiral staircase that leads to the top.

The sun has broken through the clouds since our early morning arrival and it's starting to heat up. I glance over to the seats that are occupied and see a young girl with straw-colored hair pulled back in a ponytail. My abilities tell me she's fifteen years old, but right now, she's putting out the vibe that she doesn't want to be bothered at all. The guy next to her has spikey, highlighted—come on, that's from a bottle!—blond hair and he's deep in conversation on his phone.

"Don't even think about it," Patrick quips.

"About what?"

"Him."

"Him who?"

Patrick rolls his eyes and then covers them with his sunglasses. "I saw you checking him out."

"I so wasn't." I stick my tongue out at him and then slide into one of the bench seats, patting next to me. Patrick laughs and plops down next to me, wrapping his arm around me. I feel so warm and comforted and secure. It's great that we don't have to speak so much because we each know what the other is thinking and feeling.

Well, most of the time.

Like I'm butt-crazy in love with this guy and he hasn't said that three-word phrase yet.

And I know damn well that he knows I want him to. That he…

I wince. The psychic headache is back. This time with a vengeance. Patrick notes my discomfort and holds me tighter.

"It will pass, Kendall. It's all the residual energy from all the centuries of war, battles, struggles, you name it," he tells me quietly.

I want to believe that's what it is, but there's something off. Something's not right. It's radiating all around us like a force field.

It's something…*bad.*

I try not to make a big deal out of these sensations as everyone else piles onto the bus. Taylor and Celia take the seat opposite us, while Maddie and Jessica each take a seat. Jason, with ear buds in, sits alone, three seats in front of me. It's like he's annoyed that he's here. Honestly, can't he just relax, get over himself, and have a good time?

Patrick slices his eyes over to me, obviously picking up on my thoughts. "Do you really care?"

I flatten my mouth. "Stop eavesdropping."

He rubs his chin with his thumb and forefinger. "Sorry. Hard to do sometimes."

Aunt Andi's the last one on, and she snaps her phone shut. Then, she pats my hand as she takes the bench in front of Patrick and me.

"I've never been to London. This is going to be very exciting," she says. "While you guys are doing your thing with Oliver, I'm going to scope out some of the art galleries."

I lift a brow. "Looking for stuff to take back to your gallery in St. Louis?"

"Possibly. It'll also keep me out of your hair while you're busy," she says.

"She doesn't mind you in her hair, Aunt Andi," Patrick says.

"You're so adorable," she says, making Patrick blush. She turns to glance about and sort acts like she wants to takes charge since Oliver isn't here with us. "So, does everyone know each other?"

"We're good," I say.

All the intros were done in the airport, except for the couple in the back. Although, I know deep down that they're not a *couple* couple.

I turn my attention to the blond ponytailed girl. She's really cute, but I can see that she's extremely shy, hiding behind her stylish wire-framed glasses and squinting up into the sun. The guy with her finally clicks off his phone and stares forward. The blond girl gazes up adoringly at him like she's some presidential candidate's wife out on the campaign trail. She's totally into him. Crush as big as the British Isles. And I can't blame her. The guy is... gorgeous.

He's not gorgeous in a ruggedly handsome way like Patrick or a classic high school jock way like Jason. This guy is... pretty. And he knows it. I'm easily picking up that he's been praised and placated his whole life about his good looks. Narcissism exudes from him, mixed with an over-confidence that keeps him going. His skin is tanned—a bit too much—and it looks as though he's had a slight tattoo of eyeliner. I'm not getting the vibe that he's gay or anything. Just on his own plane of existence. His golden hair is sculpted and styled and I dare any wind gust to mess it up. His eyes shift directly toward me and there's a jolt through my body. Not like I'm attracted to him or anything. (I have enough men on this trip, *thankyouverymuch.*) I am intrigued by him, though. Gray, clear, emotionless eyes cut through me, issuing a warning of sorts and pulling up a dark, black curtain of mystery around him. I try to read him, but he's mentally shut me down, blocking me from knowing any details of the who, what, where, when, why of who he is and what he's doing here.

The only polite thing to do—what my mother has taught me all of my life—is to introduce myself and be civil, since we're apparently going to be living and working together this summer.

Just as I'm about to nudge Patrick to let me up, Maddie Puckett gasps like she's just seen David and Victoria Beckham. She slides over into Andi's seat and hunkers down low to whisper to me.

"Oh, my God! Do you know who that is back there?" She's obviously star struck.

I'm figuring it's some Simon Cowell discovery I don't know about, so I shrug.

"That's *the* famous teen psychic, Christian Campbell. He's, like, all the rage on YouTube for his psychic gallery sessions over here in Europe. He uses Ouija boards to connect with spirits of the people in his audiences. I heard the BBC was looking to give him his own television show."

I ignore the pop culture aspect of his bio and instead focus on his metaphysical object of choice. A Ouija board.

A skitter of shock runs up and down the length of my spinal cord and I'm not happy about this at all. The mere thought of a Ouija board skeeves me out. Somehow, it just seems to be opening a portal that we don't need to be messing with. (And hello...didn't anyone watch *Paranormal Activity* when that mofo burst into flames? No, thank you!)

Maddie bounces in her seat in full fan-girl mode. "How amazing is *this* going to be, getting to work with *the* Christian Campbell."

"Thrilling." More than a bit of sarcasm laces my voice.

I turn to look at the celebrity in our midst.

Christian lasers his gray eyes at me and then places dark sunglasses on his face, hiding him from the rest of our group.

Ouija board use aside, there's something about this kid that screams out, "Beware of Wolf."

I wonder what we've got in store for ourselves.

CHAPTER FOUR

The double-decker bus begins to move through the early morning Heathrow traffic. I fascinated by my surroundings knowing there are rocks here in this country older than the entire United States. It's a bit overwhelming to do a quick mental flashcard review of the hundreds of battles, royal struggles, and religious melees this land has seen. The awe-inspiring location doesn't seem to affect Maddie, at all. She's more focused on gossiping about the "celebrity" in our midst.

She leans in and whispers, "I read online that Christian charges three hundred dollars for a private psychic reading, and that he's booked solid through the end of the year."

Patrick harrumphs. "Guess he doesn't have to worry about college tuition like the rest of us, huh?"

I elbow him in the ribs even though I totally agree with him.

Maddie types something into the browser on her phone. "Check this out," she says in a second. "There's a picture on his website showing him with angel wings, saying that he's 'a messenger of God.'"

I take the phone and peer at the webpage, screwing up my nose. "Hmmm, last I checked, messengers of God didn't charge three Benjamins per hour for their services." Father Mass, my Episcopal priest and friend, would be disgusted at someone using a psychic talent that God gave them for their own profit and fame.

Patrick takes the phone and scrolls around on the site. I rest my chin on his shoulder and follow along with my eyes. There are all sorts of scheduled appearances, interviews, videos, and testimonials on Christian's page. Patrick starts laughing. "Get this. He's got a disclaimer on the site. Right next to the PayPal button where you pay to schedule your three-hundred dollar session."

I snag Maddie's phone from Patrick to see this for myself:

LEGAL DISCLAIMER

Please be advised that no psychic reading can predict, forecast, diagnose, or provide information with absolute certainty. No guarantees or assurances of any kind are given and neither Christian Campbell, nor his affiliates, will not be held accountable for any interpretations, misinterpretations or decisions made by recipients based on information provided during readings.

For entertainment purposes only.

"What a piece of work," I mutter under my breath. "Entertainment, huh? He finds it entertaining to speak with the dead? To be haunted—literally—by spirits who don't know what they're doing and why they're doing it? I'd like to tell him about the ghostly bitch that pushed me down the staircase and put me in the hospital, or the possessed doll that killed my friend Farah in a car wreck, or the spirit who led us out to the woods to find her dead body after her boyfriend murdered her, or—"

Patrick calms me by tightening his arm around my shoulder. "Shhh…"

"Why use psychic abilities if you think it's only for other people's entertainment?" I ask passionately. My friends and mentors, Loreen Wood and Father Massimo Castellano told me this is a gift I've been given. A talent I have to use for good to help others. Yet this well-polished kid gets to profit from his abilities?

Maddie seems taken aback. Then again, she's one of Christian's fan-girls. "We're all into this for different reasons, Kendall. Don't wig."

"I didn't realize I was wigging," I say to my friend.

She retrieves her phone and slips back over to her seat as the bus rounds a curvy bend.

I feel a growl wanting to escape from me. Instead, I tamp it down, trying to hold in my disgust. "I'd never charge people three hundred dollars to help them with a loved one who's passed on," I tell my boyfriend through gritted teeth.

"Neither would I."

Kendall, I don't trust that guy. Not one bit.

Why?

I can't put my finger on it yet, but I don't trust him.

I don't either. But it's mostly because I don't like the way Christian's gray eyes cut through me. Even though I have my back turned to him, I sense him there. Christian Campbell is definitely trying to size me up and read me.

"That does it."

Instead of playing psychic mind games, I knock Patrick on the thigh and get him to let me out of the seat. I'm going to introduce myself to Christian and find out what his deal is.

Walking straight back to where Christian is sitting, I grip the seat back to steady myself from the bumpy ride. The young girl next to him sits up, wide-eyed as I approach. Then, she smiles sweetly at me.

"You're Kendall from America," she says in a thick Scottish brogue.

"Yeah, I am. Hi." I extend my hand to her, and when our fingers meet, I see into her mind. The small school she attends. The herd of cats at her house that she cares for and feeds. The sick grandmother she goes to visit every Tuesday and Thursday. Mostly, I see the shy fear behind her kind eyes. And, most definitely, a starstruck awe at the guy sitting next to her.

"I'm Jayne Mcburney," she says. "Oliver told us about you. I think you're one of his faves."

I release her hand and then take the seat in front of them, twisting to face the two of them. My cheeks heat slightly at the compliment, but I can't think about that right now. Christian's eyes are shielded by sunglasses and he's sitting very still and quiet. The rapid tapping inside my skull picks up again. It's as though I've nailed up boards to cover up the windows to my soul, yet someone's pounding on the outside to be let in.

That someone is clearly Christian Campbell.

He slowly draws off his sunglasses and stares me down. "You're the late bloomer, aren't you?"

I cock my head at him. "What do you mean by that?"

"Nothing. It's just that I began having psychic intuitions when I was five years old and I first saw... the beast next to my bed." He shudders and places a fist to his mouth, probably more for dramatic effect than anything else. Jayne moves her hand to comfort him. I guess she knows the story about "the beast." He peers directly at me. "Yet, from what Oliver says, you've only had psychic abilities for a matter of months."

"Since August," I snap, as though I'm defending my awakening. "It's been almost a year."

Jayne looks down and presses her glasses up her nose with her forefinger. "My visions started when I was nine. Seven years ago."

The invasive knocking continues against my brains. I tense up and glare at Christian. *Ummm... I so don't think so, dude. First off, I just met you. Secondly, not thinking you're the most honest person on the bus, and, thirdly, my boyfriend's the only one allowed to see and hear my thoughts and even that's an iffy thing.*

"I'm sure this will be an interesting summer then, Kendall," Christian says. His crisp, clipped accent nearly unnerves me.

So, I focus on Jayne, reading her mind clearly since she has no cloak surrounding her thoughts. I see green, rolling hills, a churning, dark ocean, men in kilts—mostly warriors who could stand a long, hot shower, and, most interestingly, a long, curling mist trying to shroud a secrecy hidden deep within *someone*. Not Jayne, though. "You're from Scotland," I say, not ask, with a smile. "What part?"

"Aberdeen," Jayne says with a large smile. "Have you been there?"

I shake my head. "No, this is the first time I've been out of the States."

Christian levels his eyes at me. "Of course it is."

Before I can snap his head off, Jayne tells me, "I won a contest on Christian's website to come on this trip and learn from him. I'm his protégé."

She seems like a genuinely sweet girl, but I don't think Christian Campbell's the right teacher for her awakening. What was Oliver thinking, bringing this polished piece of work on our trip like this?

A niggling in my head tells me that I need to reach out to Jayne. She seems too naïve, so innocent, and so lost. Her eyes are dilated and full of excitement and confusion. I recognize all of the emotions because I had them myself the first day I arrived from Chicago, fresh to my new home in Radisson, Georgia. And now look at me. I reach out to the girl who's only a couple of years younger than I am, yet it seems like such a bigger gap. "I'm here to help you out however I can, Jayne."

A beautifully wide smile runs across her face. "Thanks, Kendall, that's—"

"—not necessary," Christian finishes for her. Then he adds, "*Tapadh leat*" in a thick Gaelic brogue.

"Thank you," Jayne says, nodding her head at her mentor.

Okay, so that's the way it is. I understand perfectly. I leave them and move up the aisle to return to my seat.

"Is he as big of a jerk as I thought?" Patrick asks.

All I can do is harrumph.

While I've been chatting it up, our double-decker has rolled straight from the airport into the famed capital city of England. Modern building tops peek up through medieval structures, blending together in a harmonious historic architecture of what makes London one of *the coolest* places on the planet. So I've read. And now I'm here!

"You're missing the view," Patrick says to me.

"Not anymore."

Like a kid at Disney for the first time, I hang over the edge of the bus watching Londoners rushing to work this Monday morning. Lush green trees, a perfectly manicured lawn, and a reflecting lake catch my eyes. It's St. James Park. Not that I see a sign or anything; I just *know*. This is one of the most amazing things about being psychic now. I just know *all* of these historical things. I squint harder at the area and literally see the outline of the old York Palace that King Henry VIII got from his counselor, Cardinal Wolsey. (Okay, so I watched *The Tudors* on Netflix and learned some things.) But as I gaze out, the beautiful landscape turns a bit dank and dirty. There are camels, elephants, and crocodiles wandering about as though they fit naturally here.

"What the—?"

Patrick, always reading my thoughts, speaks up. "When King James I took the throne of England, he turned this place into an exotic pet display area."

"Why? I ask.

Patrick shrugs. "Because he was the king and he could."

I snicker at the thought and then my breath halts.

Did I just see the soldier from the airport watching us pass by? I shake the image out of my head, wondering who this intruder is and what he wants with me.

Mentally, I charge back up my white bubble of light. I'm not letting this soldier or Christian Campbell or any unwanted dead tenant take up residence in my mind. That's just the way it is.

"Look! It's Big Ben!" Celia calls out.

"Wicked!" Jessica shouts.

Taylor focuses her camera lens on the golden building to our right housing the infamous House of Parliament and the equally renowned Big Ben. As our bus speeds onto the bridge over the Thames, I glance over and take in the London Eye. It's hugely out of place and sticks out like a sore thumb, all mechanical and modern in a city of feudal treasures. A major fish out of water. A bit like me, I suppose.

Then the creepy chill hits my spine again, reminding me that all is not as it seems and I need to be on alert. This isn't just some happy-go-lucky European summer jaunt. There's work to do here.

The watching eye in London isn't some slow, mechanical Ferris wheel; rather, it's the polished teenager sitting behind me.

I'm going to have to guard my every move.

CHAPTER FIVE

We have seriously arrived in the lap of London luxury. Or rather, the best hotel that Oliver Bates's television reputation can buy. Which is quiet chic.

Taylor drops her bags onto the bed in our penthouse—yes... penthouse!—apartment at the Park Plaza County Hall across the river. I guess I should call it a flat, though, to get into the vernacular of my surroundings.

Maddie Puckett rushes over to push the curtains aside "Y'all! Check out the view!"

I follow the other girls and gasp when I take in the awe-inspiring skyline of London, with the Eye staring back at us. I could spend a year exploring this hotel suite alone, with the kitchen, lounge, living area, and outside balcony, but I need to snag my sleeping space first. Since Jessica and I've shared a room before, the two of us pair up in one of the bedrooms with Taylor and Celia claiming the one in the large suite, and Jayne and Maddie agreeing to share the pull-out sofa bed.

"Where's your aunt staying?" Jess asks.

"She has a room down the hall," I tell her. "She's here to chaperone and support and everything, but she doesn't want to be in my way."

Jess nods. "She's way cool. Things are looking up for you, Kendall, since our spring break."

I feel a slight blush, knowing she's talking about Patrick. "Yeah, things are great with Patrick. We were really meant to be together."

She lifts a brow at me. "And the hottie with the blue eyes?"

29

"The ex."

"That boy has a lot of red going for him," she tells me. Jessica's specialty is reading people's auras. Apparently, we're all surrounded on some ethereal level by a rainbow of color. Each meaning something different about our spirit...and our soul. "Lots of red. He's got gusto. And he's all about seizing opportunities."

I screw up my face. "Yeah, like worming his way onto this trip."

"Careful, Kendall. You're still drawn to that red aura."

Laughter bubbles from me. "Get over it, Jess."

She plops onto the bed. "I'm just saying. Once you pick up someone's red aura and they catch your attention, no matter who they are, that aggressive red aura will throw caution to the wind to pursue what they want. And that boy still wants you."

I toss my hands up. "And I'm not going there again."

Jessica grins at me. "You've got light blue shining off of you."

"Which means?"

"Just that you're spiritual, intuitive, metaphysical."

"Well, duh." I start stacking my shorts and jeans together, looking at the dresser for which drawer to take. Then I wonder. "What are you seeing from that Christian kid?"

Jessica closes her eyes for a moment and breathes deeply. "Oddly enough, he's covered in a gray and black haze."

I pop up. "I thought black meant death!"

"Not always," she tells me. "It could mean an illness or a tragedy that's befallen him. Or it could just be that he's filled with hate."

I sigh, long and hard.

Jess holds up her hand, though. "Mostly, he's gray, like I said. Which concerns me even more because variants of the color gray really say a person is secretive and self-protective. It's a wall around them saying they want to be left alone. The gray aura means they don't want to be the center of attention and really just want to fade into the background."

"Hmm, that doesn't exactly sound like a kid who's out to be the next big thing in British TV since last season's *The X Factor* winner."

"Right," Jess agrees. "Usually a predominantly gray aura means the person is a loner, not so much because they want to be, but because they're scared out of their mind. There's a lot of hurt there in him. He's looking for someone to cling to. Someone to help heal him."

I wonder if that person is Oliver? Or even Jayne? Or maybe... *me*?

After unpacking and then freshening up in the bathroom, I venture out to the large gathering area where Patrick, Jason, and Christian are lounging about. All three of them are on their phones, not even caring about their amazing surroundings.

"How's your room?" I ask, dropping down next to Patrick on the couch.

He gives me the boy shrug, not even taking his fingers off the phone screen where he's making a baby dragon fly as far from its mother as possible.

Boys.

"So, you're, like, rooming with Jason?"

"Oliver has the other penthouse for us. I'll take a couch or something. I'm not worried." Then he pauses his game and looks up at me. "Don't worry, Kendall. We won't be swapping gossib about your or who treats you better."

I gulp down the knot of emotion in my throat. There's a knock on the main penthouse door. Jayne bolts up to answer it, and I hear her squeal.

"I can't believe I'm meeting you!" she gets out in a high pitch.

"Where are my guests?" I hear, and know that Oliver has arrived.

Oliver Bates, the star of TV's *Ethereal Evidence*, strides into the room, waving at us. He looks exactly like he does on my plasma and the same as when I spent my spring break in California with him.

Jessica and Maddie both hug Oliver and the guys stand to shake hands with him. Oliver's not very tall, quite thin, and has a thick head of black hair to match his bushy mustache. That `stash is the source of his psychic "powers," meaning that whenever it begins to irritate, itch, or otherwise twitch, he's in the presence of something paranormal. I notice that as soon as he enters our presence, his hand goes straight to the edge of his facial hair and he begins to stroke it.

What is he picking up?

He turns to Christian and shakes his hand. Something seems odd between the two of them, almost as though Oliver is in awe of this kid. I roll my eyes in spite of myself.

"And there's Kendall," Oliver calls out. "Staying out of trouble?" He grins as he moves toward me, and I accept a hug from his outstretched arms.

"Now what fun would that be?"

Oliver rubs me on the head, totally messing up my freshly-brushed do. I introduce him to the rest of the gang from Radisson, all of whom seem a bit star-struck by him.

Oliver places his hands together, pressing fingertips to fingertips. "Look, kids, this is going to be an amazing summer. As you see, we'll have top-notch accommodations. I promise to feed you well, and you'll get time to be tourists and see these fabulous European cities. However, we also have a lot of work to do. People who need our help. Spirits who are lost and causing trouble. You all know what at stake."

Everyone in the suite nods, even Jason.

"I want you all to get comfortable, put your walking shoes on, and come with me to see London. Our bus is going to take us around the city, and then I've got us a lunch reservation. You have to try some incredible British cuisine."

"Fish and chips and hot beer?" Celia mutters.

I knock her with my elbow and frown.

Taylor whispers. "London is one of *the* upcoming cities for haute cuisine that infuses so many different cultures."

I giggle. "Thanks for that Food Network update, Paula Dean."

Taylor turns deep crimson and we all laugh together. I love that my girls are here with me. While I love Maddie and Jessica, they have *abilities* like me, which allow them to see the world differently. Having Taylor and Celia here, though, puts things into perspective, grounds me, and reminds me that, deep down, past the psychic abilities and ghost hunting, I'm still just... *me*..

That's me in a nutshell.

❧　❧　❧

We spend the next couple of hours being out-and-out tourists in London. The double-decker charter bus came back to take us to all of the sites in the city. I stash away worries of Jason Tillson being on the trip with his puppy dog, lovelorn looks he keeps tossing my way. And I nix any worries over the exact agenda of this Christian Campbell person. Instead, I'm just Kendall, American visitor enjoying my summer vacation. I sit on the top deck holding hands with Patrick as the historic sites whiz by us.

We'll have time later this week to actually visit some of these famed locations on our own, but for now, I marvel at everything I see. The streets are hustling and bustling, full of regular Londoners (Londiniums?) and visitors alike. The stores are packed tightly together, and each corner seems to have a pub with a lion or a crest on the sign. We pass by Trafalgar Square, then Churchill's Cabinet War Rooms (where he ran World War II from an underground headquarters), again by Parliament and Big Ben and the London Eye. This city is alive with excitement, as well as history. I glance over at the seat next to me and see that Celia's Mensa-level brain is about to explode from the overwhelming information overload. She's as much a geeky history buff as I am, and there's no better place to quench that thirst than here.

The bus stops outside of Number Ten Downing.

"What's happening?" Taylor asks.

Christian rolls his eyes and puts his sunglasses back in place, obviously bored with our expedition. But Jayne is nearly hanging off the side of the bus in anticipation. She points down.

"Look! There's a motorcade!"

We all swarm to the right of the bus and glance down. Sure enough, a few Bobbies (the London cops) have traffic stopped so a black sedan can pull out.

The tour bus driver tells us, "As you can see at Number Ten Downing, our prime minister's motorcade is exiting the location. More than likely, he's off to an important political meeting."

We see an older man step out of the residence and slip into the waiting car. Yep, that's the Prime Minister! Wicked.

Patrick snickers. "I could read him from here. He's headed to view a soccer match."

Sometimes, being psychic is literally too much information.

In any case, it's still cool. We wave and clap as the car pulls out and on its way. How many kids can say they've seen a British PM? Well… this girl.

I retake my seat, a bit breathless from the experience, but it's nothing compared to what's in store for us next. The bus twists and turns through the traffic to arrive at the looming Gothic figure of Westminster Abbey. I gasp hard at all the monarchs and rulers from London's storied past that are buried and memorialized here. But most of all, to me, it's a place where fairy tales come true. Where Prince William and Princess Kate were recently married. And where one of my favorite people of all time, Princess Diana, had her funeral. I tear up at the memory of how the world lost such an amazing figure. Of how two boys lost their mother in a vicious car wreck. Just like how mother, Emily. A car wreck that I was involved in, as well, since Emily was still pregnant with me. For some reason, I've always felt a connection to the British princess who not only touched a nation, but touched the world. As we pass by the amazing structure, it's as though I've been transported to another time, sucked into the tall, gray columns that nearly reach to the sky with their authority, making me feel insignificant in their wake.

"It breathtaking, isn't it?" I say out loud.

Patrick snaps pictures on his cell phone, and I hear nearly everyone else on the bus doing the same. The tour guide prattles on about Edward the Confessor and the Romanesque style, but I'm locked in place, breathless as I gaze at the side portal opening with cracked colors of stain glass just above it.

For standing right there waving at me with her straw colored hair swept back from her face is Princess Diana.

CHAPTER SIX

"I'm telling you what I saw," I tell Patrick sternly after we get off the bus. We've been dropped off at the location of our first case here in London's Notting Hill neighborhood. Talk about hitting the ground running.

But I'm still reeling from my ghostly encounter.

Patrick places his sunglasses on top of his head. "Kendall, I believe you *think* you saw Princess Di."

I stab my fists to my hips. "What do you mean 'think you saw Princess Di'? I know what I was looking at, Patrick. She was in a blue suit and she waved at me."

Celia's feet hit the ground with a splat. "You saw Princess Di's ghost?"

Taylor's right behind her. "I don't believe you!"

"Yeah, well neither does my boyfriend."

Patrick shakes his head. "We always see the same apparitions, Kendall. Always. I didn't pick it up. All I caught in the opening of the Abbey was a fat German guy's butt crack when he bent to pick up his map of London. No deceased royalty."

I flatten my mouth. "So, just because you didn't see it, now I'm crazy."

"No, I didn't say that." The vein in Patrick's neck protrudes, indicating his annoyance at me. "I know how much of a fan you were, and I think it was probably just residual energy— not the actual Princess."

"Oh, you think that, do you?" I don't know why I'm so irritated at him.

Jason steps in. "You know, I didn't always believe Kendall back in the beginning, but she's really good at this stuff. I say we take her word for it."

Celia's eyes widen and Taylor gasps. Jessica and Maddie know better than to stick their noses in because they can read the auras and attitudes of these two guys.

Patrick bows up and advances on Jason. It has nothing to do with my allegedly seeing Princess Di, and everything to do with these two guys scratching their rooster claws in the dirt over *me*.

Fortunately, Oliver steps off the bus and right between the two of them. "Now, now…we're here to help a client. Not fight over a girl." He smiles and nods his head. "To your respective corners."

Patrick backs off first and returns to my side. He reaches for my hands and squeezes it possessively.

What the hell is this all about?

I don't know. I don't know, Kendall.

Is something wrong with you?

Yeah, I'm not feeling myself. Something's not right. Anger is in my blood.

So, it's not about my Princess Di vision?

Patrick takes his free hand and rubs at his eyes roughly. *I don't care about that, Kendall. It's more. It's something trying to pull you away from me. I don't know if it's disguised or what.*

Out loud, I say, "You didn't get enough sleep on the plane."

He lowers his head to me. "I'm serious. We have to keep our guards up. We're not just tourists on a vacation. We're open. Spirits see us. They reach out to us. They fool us. They deceive. They manipulate. We've seen it firsthand. I swear, Kendall, I'll do everything in my power to protect you."

I lift up on my tip toes and place a kiss on his cheek.

I catch Jason watching us and then shift my eyes to see Christian watching, as well. Maybe Patrick's right. Perhaps things aren't as they appear. I just have to be careful and take care of myself.

Oliver claps his hands together. "All right, then. Now that *that's* done. We are here at the home of Mrs. Helen Flanders. She is the widow of a Royal Air Force pilot and she and her thirteen-year-old daughter have been experiencing strange occurrences in their house of late.

"Like what?" Celia asks.

"Well, let's go in and interview her, shall we?" Oliver flashes a smile.

We file up the cobblestone walkway to a lovely stone house. Mini-mansion, more like. The grass is immaculately trimmed and the hedges don't have a leaf out of place. Red, yellow, and white tulips line the flowerbeds in front of the expansive porch. A lace curtain moves back into place over the window, and I sense that Mrs. Flanders has been eagerly awaiting our arrival.

"I'm sensing something really dark in there," Maddie says to Jess and me.

I haven't picked anything up yet, but I'm still reeling from what I thought was Princess Diana waving at me. First it was the soldier in the airport and then my idol. Aunt Andi said I had to protect myself and maybe she's right. Maybe Patrick's right. I am still new to this whole psychic thing, and perhaps not-so-friendly entities on the other side—ones I've had experiences with already—are up to no good. So, I follow the group into the front foyer of Mrs. Flanders's house in an "approach with caution" manner.

The woman is very small with bright red hair and a gap in her front teeth. But her smile is genuine and almost of a relieved nature. "Oliver Bates, what a pleasure. Please do come in," she says. Then she looks at Christian and her mouth drops open. "Mr. Campbell, it's a real honor to meet you. I was at your gallery reading in Edinburgh last month."

Christian stretches his hand and takes Mrs. Flanders' in his own. "It was kind of you to invite me to your home."

Well, isn't he a little pretentious? What are the rest of us? Your fans?

Now, now…let's see how this pans out, I hear my boyfriend say inside my thoughts.

Patrick leads me into the house, squeezing my hand for reassurance.

Once inside the stately manor, we take seats throughout her living room area. The furniture is old and smells slightly of lemon Pledge or whatever the British equivalent is. She offers us a plate of cookies—or biscuits, rather—that she calls Jammy Dodgers. Jason and Patrick, of course, begin to scarf them down, but my appetite is non-existent.

Mrs. Flanders turns to Christian. "I can't tell you how relieved I am that you're here. It's been unbearable here since I connected with Alfred at your gallery reading. I do believe the old chap followed us home and isn't quite happy on the other side."

Oliver sits close to our host. "Helen, dear, please fill the rest of our team in on the recent occurrences."

Yeah, Helen, I think. *Please do.* I had no inkling that the cases we'd be working on would have involved Christian's past performances—err, readings with people. After all, his website states that what he does is for "entertainment purposes only." How is it that we are somehow here to clean up a psychic mess he conjured?

Again, Patrick squeezes my hand to calm me down.

"I do believe there's something demonic in the house," she tells us, her fingers knitting together in her lap.

"Have you seen anything?" Celia asks, much to Christian's chagrin. Maddie gasps that Celia's spoken out, glaring in my friend's direction. It's clear from the look on Christian's face that he would rather be the star of this investigation. Good for Celia for not being intimidated by his alleged celebrity star on the rise.

"We've heard pots and pans moving about in the kitchen. Just the other night, the furnace turned on and started spouting out all this thick black smoke. In the middle of the summer, can you imagine?"

Oliver tents his fingers together. "Since connecting with your deceased husband at Christian's gallery, what have you and your daughter done differently here at the house?"

The woman's mouth drops open. "That's just it. I did what Mr. Campbell suggested."

"Which was?" Oliver asks with great intent.

"Why Amberly—that's my daughter—went and purchased a Ouija board like Mr. Campbell uses in his gallery readings, and we tried to connect with Alfred right here in the house."

Disbelief coats me from head to toe at what I'm hearing. "You what?!" I shout out.

Oliver snaps his head. "Kendall!"

"No, Oliver. Those things are evil." I can hear Loreen right now telling me to stay nine miles away from them. "Why would you bring something like that into your home, Mrs. Flanders? By using something it, you're opening yourself up to possibilities that could be coming from anywhere; you don't even know."

Christian clicks his tongue at me. "Kendall, I really think you're overreacting to—"

"No, I'm not."

Mrs. Flanders acknowledges me, though. "I do agree with you a bit, love. Ever since we used that Ouija board, Amberly hasn't been herself. She's been quiet disruptive and talks back to me. We've seen items here in the house move about on their own. And then, when I threw the bloody thing into the rubbish, it reappeared in my breakfast nook. I threw it out three more times, only for it to show back up." She turns back to Christian and Oliver. "So, I'm a bit concerned."

"I don't like this at all," Jess whispers to me from my right.

"I'm not feeling well," Maddie states. "It's as though something's trying to push out of my stomach. It's the worse ache I've ever had."

Taylor stops taking pictures of the room and Mrs. Flanders so he can tend to Maddie. "Are you okay? Do we need to get you to a doctor?"

Maddie shakes her head. "No. This is what usually happens to me. Only, never like this before. Not this intense." She lifts her eyes to our leader. "Oliver?"

"Breathe through it, Maddie," he instructs. "Get in touch with your feelings and process through them. Recognize any spirit that's trying to get your attention and we'll work with them."

She nods, but I can see the fear in her eyes.

The energy in this place is dark. Damned. The walls moan out in a growl, calling to my psychic sense. Fingers of confusion curl around, trying to pit us against each other as a demonic laugh echoes throughout the house.

"Can you hear that?" I ask the group.

Jessica's eyes fill with tears. "The aura in this whole room is black."

Jayne is shaking over in the corner. "I don't like the visions I'm getting in my head."

Celia shrugs, but pulls out her KII meter to measure the electro-magnet fields in the room. "This is how I investigate." Immediately, the device in her hand lights up from green to yellow to orange, and then all the way to red. She lifts her eyes at the quick response. "Something's definitely not right here."

Mrs. Flanders covers her mouth with her hand. "Oh, dear."

"We must do a cleansing," Oliver says. "All of us are needed to pull together. We must pray hard, and use our collective energies to drive out whatever dark force has come into this house."

Mrs. Flanders inhales deeply. "You don't think it's my Alfred, do you?"

"We don't know what it is, ma'am," Patrick says kindly.

She reaches for a nearby notepad. "This was the name that was spelled out on the Ouija board both times we used it. D-o-j-o."

Christian's head snaps in her direction knowingly. "Dojo."

"Who's that?" I ask harshly.

Very dryly, Christian states, "A demon."

"Ohhhh-kay." Jason, who's been standing off in the back, sighs deeply. He levels his blue stare my way and steps forward. "*This* is what you dragged us over an ocean for? I see nothing's changed with you, Kendall. You're as senseless as ever before."

I growl at him. "No one *made* you come on this trip."

"Not now, you two," Patrick says in a hiss. "Look."

"I have this, Oliver, old chap. This is my specialty," Christian says with great calm. He snaps his fingers at Jayne, who obediently rushes to his side. "I'll take care of this."

With that, he takes the brown bag that Jayne gives him and removes a large, polished piece of lumber. It's smooth and thin and shaped like a section of a tree with ring of color showing its age before varnishing. It should be a beautiful item to behold.

It's anything but.

It's Christian's own personal Ouija board.

I gulp hard. "I don't like this one bit."

CHAPTER SEVEN

I never know when my visions or trances will hit me.

Sometimes it's when I'm just hanging out with Celia or playing with my cats Eleanor, Buckley, and Natalie, at home. Most of the time it's when I'm in deep R.E.M.

This time, it's like everything around me freezes in a stop-motion way. If someone had just come through the room, tripped, and spilled a bag of popcorn, the kernels would be dangling in the air, frozen in time while my vision comes and goes.

Slowly, I look over to my right and see my spirit guide, Anona, materialize.

She's unlike anyone I've ever seen or met in person. Of Native American decent, Anona stands before me barefoot, wearing a long, tan cloak with leather ties at the neck and waist. Her long, shiny black hair is straight and pulled to one side. Her dark brown eyes show her intense concern over what's going on here.

"Kendall, you're delving into an area you shouldn't mess with," she warns.

I shake my head, foggy almost from the daze I'm in. "I'm not doing it, Anona."

"There are dark forces at work in this universe that we don't understand."

"I don't know what you're talking about. Christian? Is he a dark force?"

She shakes her head. "That boy is a fool."

"I can't stop him," I tell her, not even feeling my lips move.

Anona spreads her arms wide. "I can't protect you against this, Kendall."

"What is it, though?"

"You've gone too far from my reach," Anona says. "There's nothing I can do."

I seriously don't get what she's telling me. My spirit guides constantly speak to me in riddles and puzzles. Why can't they just say what's on their mind? "You promised you'd take care of me."

"There is another," she says softly. "Another who is watching over you."

I perk up some from my stupor. "Emily? She's back?" I ask, almost begging. As soon as Emily, my first spirit guide, revealed herself to me as my birth mother... I lost her. She'd been with me my whole life, but as soon as I knew the truth, it allowed her to pass into the light. Great for her. Sucked for me. She'd sent Anona to be with me on the other side. But I want my mother. "Emily? Is she here again? Is she with me? Anona! Talk to me! Tell me!"

Anona brings her head down and closes her eyes, unanswering. And then she fades away.

Just like that, everything begins to move around me again, as though nothing unusual happened to me.

I have no idea how long I was out, or if anyone even noticed my spell-like state.

Patrick is over in the corner talking to Oliver. Taylor is setting up video cameras around the room. Maddie and Jess have their digital recorders out to try and capture electronic voice phenomena (EVP), while Celia is in full tech geek mode getting base readings of Mrs. Flanders's house with her EMF detector. Jason's tagging along with her, taking notes. At least he's doing something useful and helpful instead of glowering.

Christian and Jayne set up at the nearby table, with him polishing up his Ouija board as Jayne sets out the planchette—the wooden pointer used on the board.

I rub my head trying to ease the throbbing of my psychic head-ache that always follows one of my vision trips. Or maybe it's in anticipation of what's to come this evening.

The doorbell rings.

Mrs. Flanders excuses herself.

Oliver follows her.

Patrick glances over at me and smiles weakly. He knows some-thing that I can't sense.

But I don't need to, because everything's revealed when two guys bumble into the living room with a video camera and sound equipment.

"Thanks for coming so quickly," Oliver says. "We definitely want to get this on film. It'll be great for the sizzle reel we're going to pitch to the network."

Taylor's bright smile clicks into place. "We're going to be on television?"

"No way," Jess says.

Oliver twists his mustache. "Actually, I've had an idea, based on Christian's experiences here in the UK, to feature him on a new show. It's all in the development stage right now, but this is the ideal event to film and see how everything looks."

My spirit sinks and I feel myself slouch into the sofa. "So, we're just props here?"

Oliver places his hand on my shoulder. "No, no, Kendall. Do what you need to do during the investigation. I just want the cam-era crew to focus on Christian and what he's seeing, feeling, and experiencing."

Once peek over at him and I know what he's feeling. He's gaz-ing into a small mirror that Jayne's holding, checking his face and hair and dabbing a bit of pancake makeup on his cheeks.

"He's putting on makeup?" I say incredulously.

Celia plops down on the couch next to me. "What's going on here?"

"The Christian Campbell show, it looks like."

"So, Mr. Bates?" Taylor asks. "What are we supposed to do?"

"Be natural, Taylor. Just do what you always do on an investigation."

She looks over at me and shrugs. I lift my hands in defeat. It's clear that we ghost huntresses aren't needed here.

"Where shall I be?" Mrs. Flanders asks.

"I think it would be perfect if everyone gathers around the table," Christian directs. "Mrs. Flanders to my right. Jayne to my left. And the rest of you..." He trails off and syncs his eyes with mine. A slight sneer lifts the corner of his mouth. "Well, the rest of you can just fill in the spaces and not fanny about."

Celia sucks in. "Fanny about? What does that even mean?" She glares and then lowers her voice. "I don't think I like this jerk."

"It doesn't matter," I say.

Patrick comes over and offers his hand to me. "Might as well join the dog and pony show," he says with a laugh.

Everyone's in place at the table, Taylor's filming for our own purposes, but Niles and Jamie, the film crew, are set up and it's literally.... "Action!"

Christian begins using the Ouija board with Mrs. Flanders and Jayne assisting in using the planchette. It begins sliding across the slick surface passing over letters and numbers, circling back, and bringing the pointer around in circles.

In the full spotlight, Christian closes his eyes and speaks out in a booming voice. "Who is here with us tonight? Show yourself to us. Use this divination tool to come forth."

I knee Patrick under the table and he loops his fingers through mine.

This is complete crap, I say to him.

It's all for show.

"Come forth and show yourself. Who are you? Who has been terrorizing this house, this woman, her daughter?" Christian chants in a monotone.

The camera crew moves in to show Christian's hands on the planchette as it travels aggressively on the table.

D.

O.

J.

O.

"Dojo," Christian repeats. "So, it is you."

"Who is Dojo?" Jayne asks, peeping over her glasses.

Christian turns to her. "Never address a demon by name."

She shakes her head, her blond ponytail swaying. "But you just—"

Christian tosses his head back. "I am familiar with this one. He is known to me."

Oliver steps in near Christian. "Tell us what you're experiencing, Christian."

The young Scot closes his eyes again and lolls his head from left to right. Then he speaks again. "I have known you, Dojo, for years. You are the spirit that has haunted and terrorized me since I was a little boy."

I reach out with my psychic senses to see what, if anything is present or near to us. My abilities aren't picking up a thing. I don't know if that's because there's nothing here and Christian's just a big tool bag, or if this Dojo person is focused on his demonic task.

Christian's eyes fly open and he screams out. He grabs the Ouija board and lifts it over his head, shaking it fiercely. Mrs. Flanders covers her head in protection and Jayne dives under the table. I watch as Christian falls back into the chair and starts flailing about.

"You can't have me. You never have. I-I-I..." Christian slams the board to the table and then flops back into the chair, like he's passed out.

I stifle the desire to laugh, as does Celia. Instead, we watch the floor show.

Then Christian rises, and in a voice that's nothing like his thick Scottish brogue, he says, "I am Dojo. You have called me and I have come."

"Oh, dear," Mrs. Flanders says on the verge of tears. "Are you the one who has been causing trouble here?"

"I am," Christian says deeply. "I am Dojo. You summoned me. Now, what do you want?"

Oliver looks at our host. "He's doing what we call channeling, Mrs. Flanders. He's allowed this spirit to overtake him and speak through him so we can communicate."

She blinks hard and looks around the table. "Oh, well, then."

"I am Dojo. You have crossed me. You have empowered me. I shall never leave you. Just as I have ruled over this boy since his birth. His power comes from me. Dojo."

No one in the room moves. Not even the sound guy trying to stretch the boom mike in. From what I'm picking up, my friends don't know whether Christian is the real thing or if he's just crazy out of his mind.

I think it may be a recipe that includes both ingredients.

CHAPTER EIGHT

Christian screams out in pure terror, a shrilling shriek that would peel paint off the wall. Mrs. Flanders staggers away, and all of us slide back from the table. The camera man is fearless, and has the lens right up in Christian's face. Until the young psychic swipes his arm around in a kung fu chop to the left, knocking the expensive recording equipment out of Niles's hand.

Olive moves in, placing hands on both sides of Christian's head. He holds him tight and begins to whisper close to Christian's ear. "Come back, Christian. Kick him out. Take back control."

Slowly, Christian comes to and I let out the breath I've been holding. As does nearly everyone else in the room.

"What happened?" he asks, slightly dazed.

Jayne pops up from underneath the table. "You were channeling that guy whose name I'm not supposed to repeat."

Celia slides her sketch pad and charcoal pencil down the table. "Can you draw this Dojo clown for us?"

Man, I love her tenacity.

"Aye, I can," Christian says. "I've seen him my whole life."

He nabs the pencil and begins to move it quickly over the paper. Stokes and circles, lines and angles. He's obviously done this before. When he flips the book around, I yelp out. For looking back at me is a troll-like creature with a snake-ish face, eyes that hiss and stare out and a body similar to what most science fiction movies use to depict aliens.

Mrs. Flanders puts her hand to her heart and I fear for her health. "Th-th-that is in my house?"

Olive slaps the drawing down and puts a comforting hand on Mrs. Flanders's shoulder. "I believe that's enough for one night, my dear. We'll take our equipment, review our evidence, and then regroup with you. How's that?"

With a shaky hand, she reaches out to Oliver and holds on. "I suppose I'll have Father Andrew come over and bless the house tonight before I retire."

"Good idea," Oliver says.

I only pray that Christian made all that stuff up and that this poor woman isn't in any danger.

⚜ ⚜ ⚜

That night, back at the hotel, Oliver has a bounty of food sent up from room service. I barely pick at the burger and fries on my plate, still trying to grasp what happened a few hours earlier. Christian set off for the gym and has been in full work out mode since. Apparently, it's how he "relaxes" after an intense channeling session.

Maddie disappeared to call her boyfriend back home and Jessica, Taylor, and Celia talked Aunt Andi into venturing out for a ride on The Eye.

I don't know where Jayne disappeared to. I worry about her and her connection—her attachment—to Christian. That kid isn't right, and I hate to see her dragged down along with him.

I push aside the half-eaten plate of food and reach for a can of soda. As I open it, I feel warm hands on my shoulder.

"Hey, babe," Patrick says. "No appetite?"

"Not really."

"I know what you need," he says. "Come with me."

A naughty part of me giggles in delight over getting to spend some alone time with my boyfriend. We take the elevator down to the second floor out to an open-air terrace that overlooks the balmy London summer night.

"Oh, wow, this is gorgy," I exclaim.

"They just opened this patio up a couple of years ago. They call it The Urban Garden."

Looking about, there are lounge chairs, chaises, and an area to watch TV on the large screen. Most of all, there's a small, white-draped tent overlooking a view of neighboring buildings and the London Eye off in the distance.

"It's perfect," I say. "Let's make it our place while we're here in London."

Patrick pulls me to him, wraps his arm around my back, and places a kiss on my lips. He's so warm and strong and I just want to disappear into the moment. His mouth is firm on mine and I move my lips to enjoy the feel of him so close.

"Mmm…," I say when we pull apart.

"I've missed that," he whispers into my hair. "We've been too crazed. I needs me some Kendall time."

I laugh and hug him tightly. "And I needs me some Patrick time."

A gentle breeze dances over us as we start kissing again. Nothing naughty or inappropriate, just being with the guy I'm crazy about and trying to block out the events of the evening.

Patrick pulls back, though. "Crap."

"What?" I wonder what's happened now.

"My phone's ringing." He dives into his pocket and activates the screen.

"Let it go to voice mail," I beg.

Patrick's eyes grow big. "It says Kennesaw Hospital." He clicks on the phone. "Hello? Yes, this is Patrick Lynn."

Silence.

He listens.

So do I, in his mind.

His father's in the emergency room. Kidney stones that have to be removed.

"Oh, Patrick!"

He holds up a hand to silence me. The person on the other end of the call continues. Patrick covers the phone and I hold his hand.

I'm transported into the call where I hear that his dad is going to be okay. No need for Patrick to return home. Selfishly, I'm relieved. There's no way I can deal with Christian Campbell's machinations without Patrick by my side.

"He's going to be fine," Patrick says, hanging up.

He lowers himself into a chair and puts his head in his hands. I won't let him wallow, though, so I pull him to me. He moves his head to my stomach and wraps his arms around me. A long, exhausted sigh escapes him and I gently rub at his head, combing my fingers through his thick, brown hair.

"I'm so tired," he mumbles into my shirt.

"You should get some rest," I say.

His wide yawn is evident of his state of mind. "So much for Patrick and Kendall time, huh?"

"It's okay. It was only our first day here." It's too peaceful of a night to go to sleep yet. "I'm just going to sit here for a bit and take it all in."

He lifts up and pulls me to him again, placing a big smooch on my forehead. "You'll be okay?"

"I'm fine. Get some sleep."

Like a zombie, he wanders off, waving at me.

"Love ya, mean it," I call out, but I don't think he heard me. There's an actual ache in my chest thinking of the words that I usually toss out at most everyone. Thing is, I do love him. Like, big time. Every moment with him, each experience ...only pulls me closer to him. A love deeper and more meaningful than what I felt for...

"All alone out here?" Jason asks from behind me.

I jump a bit, disappointed that I hadn't felt his presence before he showed himself. "Patrick just went to bed."

Jason bobs his head and advances toward me. He's wearing tan shorts and a light blue shirt that I can tell matches his eyes, even in the darkness of the London night. "It's quite an adventurous path our summer trip has taken already. Never a dull moment in the life of psychic, Kendall Moorehead."

He's too close. I need to make space. I crawl into one of the large vinyl chairs and pull my feet up on the edge. Then I wrap my arms around my legs and rest my chin on my knees, trying to fold up into the smallest space possible.

"You don't have to worry about me anymore, Jason."

He runs his hands through his hair and then sits down next to me. Stupid boy. Can't read my body language, eh? "Oh, I think I'll always worry about you, Kendall. Even when I was in Alaska, I thought of you."

I can't help but harrumph at this admission. "Whatever, Jason."

He looks out over the skyline and traces his finger in the air where the outline of The Eye is spinning slowly. "It's not whatever, Kendall. Because you're still dragging my sister into your dramas. Over and over again. Like tonight at that lady's house. What was that all about?"

I bolt straight up, my feet thwacking on the deck floor. "Give me a break! Taylor is part of my team and she was *invited* to participate in some pretty important ghost hunting cases this summer. *You're* the one who merely came along for the ride."

"Taylor's not as strong as you."

"So says you."

"She can't handle this stuff."

"Taylor's fine," I insist.

"But will you be?" Jason turns to me, concern painted all over him. "Come on, Kendall. A demon named Dojo with the head of a snake and the body of an alien. Really? Is this why we're in Europe? Dealing with bullshit like this?"

I point my finger in his face. "I've dealt with a lot of paranormal crap since you've been gone, Jason. I've helped a lot of spirits who were lost and stuck and missing. This is no different. I'm doing this because it's what I'm meant to do."

Shaking his head, "You're going to wind up hurt."

"No, I'm not."

A long sigh escapes from him. "I can't deal with this."

I grind my teeth together and then say, "I have no idea why you're here at all."

Swiftly, Jason takes me by both shoulders and shakes me a bit—not in a bad way at all. "I'm here because I still care about you, Kendall. I've missed you so much. I can't stop thinking about you. I hate myself for losing you. There!"

Shock rocks me from head to toe. There was a time when I would have melted in a puddle at his feet just to hear him utter those words. Now, I'm way too stunned to move or speak or breathe or think.

Jason draws me to him and his grip turns to a caress. "I still love you, Kendall."

He what?

Before I can breathe or even comprehend the meaning, the atmosphere around us shifts. Heated energy crackles around us and I can't move. Paralyzed by the jolt of his admission. He still loves me? He hates himself for losing me?

Jason angles his head to the right and moves in for the kill. Then I feel his lips on mine—only for a second—and then an explosive bombshell zips through me, surprising me enough to push him back and jump to my feet.

I wipe away his kiss with the back of my hand. "Are you kidding me? You can't do that."

Jason's eyes blaze with a passion I've never seen from him before. "I can't kiss you?"

"No! These lips don't belong to you anymore. I'm with Patrick. Deal with that, Jason!"

Then I shove him. Hard. Like Wonder Woman strength hard. Like someone else is helping me hard.

"Kendall! Don't!"

I run past him straight for the elevator.

I'm not aware of pushing the penthouse button, yet somehow I manage to do it.

Key card in the lock, jerk the door open, and flee into the bathroom.

Immediately, I twist on the cold water and begin to splash my face. A cool awakening that washes away what just happened. Or, at least I hope it does. I don't like how his kiss made me feel. Missed. Appreciated. *Loved.*

Slamming my hands to the countertop, I glare at my reflection. "*That* will never happen again."

CHAPTER NINE

After a night a whole hell of a lot of tossing and turning, I reach for the teapot and fill my cup up with a second helping of English breakfast to help bring me into the real world.

"*Bonjour!*" Taylor sings out as she takes a seat at the table next to me in our penthouse suite. A bountiful breakfast has been delivered and is spread out before us. She reaches for a plate and heaps on scrambled eggs, slices of ham, and buttered toast. "I have never slept so wonderfully in my life. It's like that mattress wrapped its arms around me and hugged me all night."

I groan inwardly, but smile at my friend. "I'm glad someone rested." I scoop out some eggs onto my own plate and reach for a roasted tomato to go along with it.

"Were you thinking about what happened at Mrs. Flanders's house?" she asks.

No, I was thinking about your stupid brother.

"Among other things," I answer.

Taylor pats my arm gently. "I'm sure we'll be able to help her out. We always help out."

Jessica, Celia, Jayne, and Maddie wander in and we all dig in to the breakfast feast and the chatter about last night's investigation continues. I sip—gulp actually—my tea hoping the caffeine kicks in quickly. Anything to tamp down all of my nerves and restlessness. There's an overall icky sensation covering me that I know is more than just Jason Tillson putting the moves on me. It's something from the other side reaching out to me, only I don't know who or what it is. Could it be this other person who's watching after me, as Anona told me? Honestly, why do these spirits have to be so vague?

The door to our suite opens and in walks Oliver, followed by Patrick, Jason, and Christian.

"Good morning," Oliver says to us all. "Pip-pip, cheerio, and all those other English quips."

"Hey, Oliver," we all sing out in unison.

Patrick comes up and hugs me from behind, planting a kiss on the top of my head. His hair is all boy-messy from sleep and he's got this sexy stubble on his face like he doesn't care. "Hey, babe."

I don't even look at Jason, although I can feel his eyes on me. Christian, too, seems to be watching me. What is it with these guys? Do they all have to be so... overwhelming?

Patrick fills a plate with a heaping serving of everything on the table and then sits down opposite from me. I concentrate on surrounding myself thoroughly with the white light to protect my thoughts and feelings. The last thing I want is for Patrick to tap into my memory of last night's debacle.

Oliver sets down his briefcase and reaches for a croissant and lets out a long sigh. "I'm afraid I have some bad news."

Christian sits to his right and seems as if he already knows what Oliver's going to say. A smug assuredness overcomes him and I don't trust him as far as I could throw him.

"What's up?" Celia asks, speaking up for the group.

Oliver clears his throat. "We won't be going back to Mrs. Flanders's house."

"Why not?" I blurt out.

"That's fine with me," Jess says.

Jayne nods quietly.

"After we left last night," Oliver says, "she contacted her Anglican priest. He was none too pleased that she'd allowed 'a bunch of spook hunters' into her house and he accused us of 'stirring up the devil.'"

"That's ridiculous," Patrick says.

"I agree," Jess says, darting her eyes around.

I set my tea cup down. "But Oliver, it's clear there's something haunting her house. They've had poltergeist activity, and I'm sure once we review the recordings from last night, we'll find EVP to back that up."

He holds up his hand. "Kendall, I understand, but Mrs. Flanders won't allow us back anymore. Her priest did a blessing on the house and that's that."

"What did she do with the Ouija board?" Maddie asks.

Oliver reaches over for his discarded briefcase, sets it on the table, and pops it open. Slowly, he withdraws the Ouija board that Mrs. Flanders had in her house. I gasp, as do the other girls. Jayne, in particular, shudders a bit. The young girl is definitely frightened, but she remains quiet.

"What are you going to do with that?" Celia asks.

Christian just snickers. "I'll take it, Oliver. It's been calling out to me ever since last night, so I think I should add it to my collection."

I'm not crazy about the notion of one Ouija board in our presence, much less two. But that's just me.

Oliver hands the item over to Christian. The young psychic stares directly at me, trying to penetrate my thoughts which I've thankfully guarded.

Then, he says, "Mark my word. We haven't heard the last of Dojo this summer."

⚜   ⚜   ⚜

After another full day of playing tourist—watching the changing of the guards at Buckingham Palace, climbing to the top of St. Paul's Cathedral, and taking a boat ride down the Thames—there's no time left to hash about the men who've invaded my life. Patrick's in historical geek mode as we tour around, Jason's hanging out with Celia who's giving him her own narration of the city, and Christian is pensively hanging in the wings, seemingly bored with the architecture and antiquity of his own country. I stick with the girls, snapping photo after photo of all the great sites and posting them immediately to my Facebook page for everyone back home to see.

Now, after a quick dinner at a friendly neighborhood pub, we've arrived via our chartered double-decker bus in the Kensington area of London, where our next investigation awaits us.

Lady Margaret Hewitt, a ginormous fan of Oliver's, greets us as we file into her gorgeous home. Actually, it's more like a small castle in the middle of the city.

"Aren't you teenagers adorable. I'm so honored to have you here in my home. And Oliver, you're my favorite psychic on the telly."

Oliver actually blushes at her compliment. "Now, Lady Hewitt, you do go on."

"How old is your house, Lady Hewitt?" Celia asks in full investigative mode.

"The land has been in my family dating back to the fifteen hundreds," she says proudly. "I've been here for thirty-nine years."

"What sort of paranormal activity have you been experiencing?" Maddie asks.

Lady Hewitt takes a handkerchief from her pocket and dabs her pale, white skin. It's apparent there's something causing the noble woman to perspire just thinking about what's disturbing her home.

"There are what you'd call cold spots abounding in the house. Not just in the winter time when a chill is expected. Rather, in the middle of summertime. Like this morning. I was sitting down to my breakfast and my maid told me the pantry in the kitchen was ice cold. I stepped away from the dining room and followed her to find that, indeed, she was not exaggerating. I could see my breath when I walked into the storage space. Then, I experienced the same thing in the sitting room later this morning."

"It was in the nineties today," Jessica notes.

"No kidding," says Jayne.

I want to chalk up the cold spots to this simply being a drafty, stone building, but my psychic tingling senses tell me there's something more here. A presence that's watching and lurking. I spread my hands out wide and shut my eyes, opening myself up to whatever is here and whoever will communicate with me. Patrick is by my side immediately and takes one of my hands in his.

I feel it too, he tells me.

Is something following us?

Not us. Him.

I open my eyes and glance across the room. Christian is sitting in a large velvet chair staring off at nothing. He appears to be in a trance that has Oliver and Lady Hewitt completely fascinated.

"Let's do some EVP work," Celia suggests.

"I'll set up my cameras," Taylor adds.

As our team settles into the sitting room, Oliver lowers the lights. Taylor clicks on the infrared illuminator lights on her video camera so the night vision can record our investigation. Jason plops down into a chair and holds a digital recorder that Celia has given him. At least he's participating and not being a bump on a log, like usual.

Patrick squeezes my hand and smiles at me. "You okay? Ready for this?"

"Yeah, I'm fine."

But it's a lie. Not a deliberate one. Immediately, my psychic headache begins to pound out in my temple. It's as though it's rush hour in my veins and all the blood is zooming to be anywhere else right now. I wince. I cringe. I shudder.

"No, you're not fine," Patrick says quietly. He places his finger under my chin and lifts my eyes to his. I meet his dark brown gaze and nearly want to melt at the concern pouring from him.

"There's someone here."

He nods. "I feel it too."

Over his shoulder, I begin to see an apparition materializing. First, I see it's the figure of a woman, thin and tall. Next, I notice blond hair framing a beautiful ivory profile. Distinctive nose. Noble chin. She comes into full view standing next to Lady Hewitt's fireplace.

I nearly choke on my gasp. "It can't be…"

Patrick turns. "I don't see anything."

I'm overcome with a sudden awe as I swear I'm staring at the ghost of the deceased Princess Diana of Wales. I want to be a professional. I want to remain calm and in investigative mode, but I can't do it.

"Holy shit!" I exclaim, getting everyone's attention. "You guys, you won't believe this, but Princess Di is standing right over there." I point at the fireplace.

The ghost turns her head and smiles directly at me with her prim mouth turned up at the corner.

"No way!" Celia shouts as Taylor flips her camera to focus on the mantle.

Lady Hewitt inhales quickly. "The princess did live just over the way in Kensington Palace. I had the pleasure of meeting her once when she was out strolling with her boys. Lovely woman. What a tragic loss for England."

"But she's right here!" I say, geeking out.

"Talk to her, Kendall," Oliver advises.

Patrick laughs and nudges me ahead toward the specter.

Not knowing how to react, I curtsey. The ghost chuckles at me and covers her mouth with her hand. "Thank you," she says.

"Oh, my God, Princess Diana. I'm, like, a huge fan of yours. I'm so in awe of everything you did in your life, especially all of the charity work."

The ghost dips her eyes demurely at the compliment as the rest of the team surrounds me with camera and digital recorders.

"Are you in pain?" I ask.

"No, dear."

"What happened that fateful night in Paris? In the Pont de Alma tunnel?"

She doesn't respond.

I push, though. "You died in a horrible car accident."

The princess nods. "The accident happened very quickly. My pain has been forgotten."

From across the room, Christian apparently can't stand that I'm conversing with a famous British ghost. He tugs out one of his

Ouija boards and crosses over to where I am. He sits down on the floor in front of where the princess is standing and lays the board on the floor.

"Jayne, I need you," he says calmly. She scuttles over quickly and sits next to him.

Incredulously, I say, "I'm sort of in the middle of a conversation here, Christian."

He doesn't care or even acknowledge me. Instead, he places his hands on the planchette as Jayne does the same. "I'd like to communicate with the spirit that is here with us this evening."

Patrick steps up. "Dude, Kendall's talking to the spirit right now. Back off."

Oliver puts his hand to Patrick's chest to stave him off. "It's okay, Patrick. Let's see what Christian has in mind."

I look at Princess Di who doesn't seem amused by this. "Don't let him do this," she says firmly.

"What choice do I have?" I say back to her.

The planchette moves underneath Christian and Jayne's fingers, sliding left and right. Glancing at Maddie, I see tears filling her eyes and she begins to tremble.

"This isn't right," she whispers, but no one seems to care.

Christian closes his eyes and rolls his head around, performing, this time, for Taylor's video camera. She zooms in on him, not missing a moment, and he definitely starts to put on a show.

"Come speak to me," he says in a monotone. "You may use my body as a vessel to communicate with us. Who are you? Who is this spirit that dwells in Lady Hewitt's home?"

I reach for Patrick's hand again and lace my fingers through his. Our psychic energy surges together and I'm nearly lightning-bolted in place. An unseen vortex of cold air encircles us, swirling around and down, over toward Christian and Jayne seated on the floor.

"I call upon you to tell us your name," Christian says.

I watch, wide-eyed, as the planchette moves rapidly across the polished wood. Just as it did last night at Mrs. Flanders's house.

Celia announces, "D. O. J. O. Dojo." She snaps her head up. "It says Dojo again."

Maddie begins to cry. "I don't like this. Oliver, I'm frightened."

He shushes her. "It's okay."

No, it's not okay.

Christian's hands fall off the planchette and he flops backward onto the antique carpet. Lady Hewitt nearly spasms with her quick intake of breath. Christian jerks to the left, then the right, and squirms around on the carpet.

I honestly want to laugh in a sick sort of way. Is this kid for real?

Patrick steps in front of me almost to provide a barrier between me and Christian's shenanigans. Still, Christian shouts out in pain, writhing about. I steal a glance at Princess Di who fades away into a mere wisp of a cloud. Even she isn't impressed with the goings on here.

Then Christian screams out. "I am Dojo! The dark and evil lord. You will not cross me."

Jayne cries and backs away from Christian as fast as she can. Still, he continues channeling.

"I am the demon Dojo. You will bow down and worship me!"

A large oil painting over the fireplace crashes forward, falling to the floor where the princess once stood. Patrick and I jump back as the frame barely misses us.

"Get out!" Christian shouts. "Get out of my sight!"

Jessica and Maddie cling to each other, both of them crying hard. Celia reaches for Jason, who wraps his arm around her. Taylor, God love her, keeps a steady camera on the action.

Jayne covers her ears with her hands and screams out, "Christian! Stop this! You're scaring me!"

"I am Dojo! I am the lord demon. Worship me now!"

I break free from my boyfriend and grab Oliver's arm. "You've got to put a stop to this! Everyone is freaking the freak out."

Lady Hewitt agrees, "I do believe the young woman is right. This is way beyond what I expected when I agreed to let your group in for an investigation."

"I do apologize, Lady Hewitt," Oliver says. "We never know what we'll encounter." He bends down to touch Christian, who rears up and smacks at Oliver. Christian's fist connects squarely with Oliver's right eye and we all gasp.

"Oh, my God!" Celia shouts.

"Help him!" I add.

"I can't handle this." Maddie rushes out of the room, Jessica right on her heels.

Patrick looks over at Jason. "Help me!"

I stand back as the two of them grab Christian from either side. Oliver, shaking off the attack, places his hands on Christian's face. "Come back, Christian. Kick him out. Take your body back."

Reaching down, I grab the Ouija board and sling it across the room, away from Christian. Jayne cowers on the floor in front of me, so I stoop to wrap my arms around her. She whimpers in my ear and I whisper that it'll be okay. I hope I'm not lying.

Christian tries to take a swing at Jason, but he holds on tightly. As does Patrick. It's nice to see these two working together instead of against each other. The three men continue to wrestle around, with Oliver doing his best to bring Christian out of the trance.

And then, just like that, Christian pops back to reality, his breath ragged.

Patrick helps Jason up, and then Jason offers Christian his hand. The young Scot refuses the assistance and stands up on his own, wiping his hands down the side of his jeans. He crosses the room and retrieves his precious Ouija board, tucking it back into his bag. Jayne shivers in my arms as I hug her tightly to me.

"Why don't you go on out to the bus," I suggest. "Taylor, walk Jayne out?"

"Of course," she says. She gets her camera and then ushers Jayne out of the room.

Lady Hewitt nearly faints over onto her couch and then begins crying. "I want you out of here, straight away."

Oliver tries to catch his own breath. "I understand. We're very sorry, Lady Hewitt."

I don't blame her one bit. This was completely out of hand.

As we're leaving the castle, Christian and I are the last ones out. He levels his icy-gray stare at me as a sneer crosses his face.

"That went quite nicely, don't you think?"

He's completely out of control.

Chapter Ten

Back at the hotel, I sit out on my balcony overlooking the city and try to call Father Mass.

"How many hours am I ahead of Georgia?" I ask to no one. The time change has me completely messed up. I don't know if I'm going to wake the father up or interrupt him during a church service.

Neither. The call goes to his voice mail.

"You've reached the voice mail of Father Massimo Castellano. Please leave a message at the tone and God bless."

Beep.

I take a deep breath. "Hi, Father Mass. It's me, Kendall, calling from across the pond. How British of me, huh?" I giggle at my nervousness. "Listen, things are, like, really weird here. There's this kid from Scotland who's an up-and-coming TV-wannabe psychic and he's into using a Ouija board during our investigations. Both times he's connected with this alleged demon named Dojo that's been haunting him since he was a little kid. I don't know if he's for real of if this is all a bunch of hooey, but I just wanted to let you know. Maybe you and Loreen can help us figure out what's going on." I pause and catch my breath. "Miss you guys. Call me or e-mail. Thanks."

I click the phone off and stare out at the London skyline.

I call out to the sky. "Anona, I sure wish you'd help me. I don't know whether this Christian guy is for real or what."

I hold my breath a full twenty seconds hoping my spirit guide will appear to me. But nothing. Damn ghosts... don't show up when you really need them.

Although *someone* joins me.

"Hey, Kendall," I hear a small voice.

I turn to see the young blond push her glasses up higher on her nose. "Hey, Jayne. What's up?"

She sits next to me and fiddles with the hem of her shirt. "I wanted to thank you for helping me tonight."

"No worries," I say.

"I'm still new to all of this and it's a bit frightening experiencing things. I'm a bit scattered over my emotions and trying to sort them all out," she says in her thick Scottish accent. "I used to watch *Most Haunted* all the time, but I never thought I'd be actually going on ghost hunts myself until I started seeing ghosts."

Reaching out for her hand, I say, "I'm still getting used to all of this myself. Unfortunately, there's really no learner's manual to tell us how to think, feel, act, or whatever. We just have to figure it out as we go along."

"Right-o," she says. "You were brilliant tonight."

I shrug. "Not exactly."

"And don't you think Christian was brilliant, too?"

Not exactly. "To be honest with you, Jayne, I'm not sure what I think of Christian."

Her eyes widen. "He's amazing. He's so strong and confident. I want to be poised like him. I'm so bloody lucky to have won this chance to study with him. But even more so, I get to know all of you, as well."

I don't want to bust this girl's flavor over my own intuition about Christian. Instead, I reassure her. "I'm here for you any time you need me. We're going to be together all summer, so whatever I can do to help."

She smiles brightly. "That's fantastic." Then she closes her eyes for a second and opens them again. "I just had a psychic flash. Patrick is in the Urban Garden meditating. I think he had a lousy day."

"We all sort of did. I think I'll go see him."

I stand up to leave and Jayne grabs my hand again. "You're the best, Kendall."

✤　✤　✤

Patrick's sitting under the garden tent with his eyes closed, strumming out a Beatles tune on his guitar—appropriately so considering where we are—when I find him. I unobtrusively tug out a chair and ease down into it beside him.

He must sense my presence because he cracks open his left eye and peers over at me. A weak smile crosses his face and he stops playing.

"Hey, you," I say. "Sounds nice."

"The boys from Liverpool."

"And a little alone time for you," I add.

"Yeah, I needed it," he says. "Things aren't right."

I sigh. "I know. I've been all tingly today. And that experience with Princess Diana tonight. That was just... wow. I have no other words."

He sets the guitar down on the table in front of him and cricks his neck. "I don't know, Kendall. Maybe this trip wasn't a good idea. I thought we'd have fun, but this is...*intense*."

I want to reach out to him, but his body language isn't exactly open at the moment.

"Do you think that was seriously the Princess of Wales I saw tonight?"

"There's no telling. This land is wrought with spirit activity. And we were near where she used to live."

Dreamily, I say, "I've so admired her and have cried over YouTube videos of her funeral with those two little princes walking behind her casket. The whole world mourned for her. What an amazing soul to have affected so many people. I just don't want to think of her spirit being restless."

Patrick turns to me. "I'm sort of blown away by it, too, even though I didn't see her. Maybe it's another spirit reaching out to you *as* her."

I cock my head to the side. "Is that possible?"

Another boy shrug. "I don't know. We're still sort of learning all of this as we go along."

"Tell me about it."

We sit in silence for a moment, listening to the city sounds around us. A police siren. Cars passing underneath. Voices from a nearby balcony. The smell of Korean Pho from a street food truck. Somewhere nearby, a television sounds out the BBC's evening broadcast. A rumble of thunder overhead signals an oncoming shower.

Relaxing for nearly the first time today, I let my guard down. Curtain-falling the white light I've kept so tightly around me. So much so that I haven't even let Patrick in. I miss my connection with him, though.

I slide my hand up his arm, up onto his shoulder, and slip my fingers into his thick hair. He turns his dark eyes onto me and smiles.

"I love being here with you," I say in a whisper.

"Me too," he agrees. "I'm sorry I've been closed off. My intuition has me all jittery. And I'm worried about my dad, too."

Kneading at his neck, I ask, "He's doing okay, right?"

Patrick nods. "Yeah. He's good. I just hate that I'm not there for him. Especially when he didn't leave my side after my diving accident."

Patrick nearly died when he was diving in Barbados with his dad and got his regulator caught. He panicked and sliced the hose with his dive knife, nearly drowning before he was revived. That's when he awakened with his own psychic abilities. And now, we're totally connected with each other, so much so, that I can literally feel his heartache right now.

I want to ease his pain and let him know how much I love him, even though neither one of us have voiced the actual words.

"You're dad's a great guy," I say.

"He really likes you," Patrick says, his eyes glancing down at where our fingers are entwined.

I giggle. "And so do you."

He laughs and squeezes my hand. "Yeah. Whatever."

I reach up and tug at his hair over that comment and he yelps.

He pulls me into a bear hug and wrestles around with me for a moment as I squeal like the girl that I totally am. Then he gets still and serious, lifting his hand to cup my face. He's got that dreamy look in his eyes that he gets right before he moves in to kiss me.

And I *want* him to kiss me. I need him to kiss me.

As he moves in slowly, I turn my head and suddenly a memory of another kiss slips into my thoughts. I try desperately to block the recollection, but it's too late, and it transfers to my psychic boyfriend's mind.

He jolts back and pushes away from me. Horror and disgust cover his face. "You *kissed* Jason Tillson? Right here?"

"No!"

"Yes!"

"Patrick, I can explain! It wasn't—"

He waves me off. "You don't have to explain, Kendall. I can *see* it." Then he wipes at the air between us. "God, I don't want to see this."

I reach out for him. "It wasn't me. It was all him."

"Right."

"I pushed away from him, Patrick."

He glowers at me. "You know, I was cool with him being on this trip because I know how protective he is of Taylor. But, I've had my doubts about his motives from day one when it comes to you. I've never trusted him." Patrick's eyes sear with mine. "Apparently, I can't trust you, either."

"That's completely unfair! I can't control another person, Patrick."

"You can control yourself."

He did *not* just go there. "I didn't do anything! He kissed me."

"It must've meant something, Kendall." Patrick lightly taps his finger on my head. "I saw the memory. It's in there. You want it in there."

I shake my head, hoping it will knock that memory out onto the floor where it'll roll away into the darkness of the night.

"He does still have feelings for me," I admit honestly.

"That's apparent," Patrick says.

"I don't still have feelings for *him*," I stress.

"That is *not* apparent."

I slam my hand down. "God, Patrick! Why are you being so stupid? Boys can be so stupid." I want to tell him I love him. I want to say those three words. He can obviously hear them in my mind. Why won't he say them? Why should I have to say them first? "You have to trust me. Jason and I are over."

"I want to believe that."

"Well, believe it."

We sit in silence momentarily. I can almost hear the second hands ticking away on some unseen clock. My heartbeat picks up to a near in-need-of-medication pace.

Then I think, *I love you...*

And nothing.

Patrick slowly stands up and sulks off.

"You can't walk out on me," I beg.

"Yeah, I can." He sighs and stares at the ground. "Today was exhausting. I'm worried about Jayne and her attachment to Christian. I think Christian's a dick, and I just don't feel as bonded and connected to you since Jason Tillson came back to Radisson."

I stand up and face him. "You're the most important thing to me. None of those things matter, Patrick. You and I are the only thing that matter."

Please believe me!

Silence.

Patrick shakes his head and leans over to grab his guitar. Without speaking another word—verbally or psychically—he leaves me standing there as he heads off to his room.

The thunder booms again and the rain begins to spray down on me.

All I can do is stand here and get soaked.

Chapter Eleven

I'm shaken awake by a loving hand.

"Come on, Kendall. Time to get up," Aunt Andi says.

"I don't want to," I mumble from underneath the covers. "I had a crappy night."

She mercilessly pulls the blanket away from me. "But you're going to have a wonderful day."

I tuck my head under the mountain of pillows and moan. My head hurts from overthinking everything that's happened since I touched down here in the United Kingdom. My eyes ache from crying myself to sleep after Patrick walked out on me. "London sucks."

My aunt cracks up laughing at me and then climbs up onto the mattress. The allegedly mature adult that's supposed to be my responsible chaperone begins to jump up and down on the bed like a kid away at camp for the first time.

Bounce.

Bounce.

Bounce.

"Get up, Kendall!"

My sensibilities are being jostled around like chicken in a Shake and Bake bag. I grip the headboard for stability while my aunt continues her attempt to woman-handle me out of bed.

"Andi! Stop it!" She lands flat on her bum next to me and rolls over, dog-piling me with her weight. "How old are you?"

She laughs at me. "Come on, sweetie. Oliver's giving you guys the day off. You've been working too hard and not getting the chance to enjoy this amazing city. And for that matter, neither have I. I've been scoping out art galleries and talking to artists and photographers. I need some girl time with my favorite niece."

I turn into her outstretched arms and accept the warm, inviting hug. She's the closest thing I have to my living biological family and I find that I love her deeply. She pets my unruly mess of sleep-mussed hair and I feel a deep ache in my throat, constricting an emotional lump that threatens to bring on tears. Okay, so it does bring on tears. I sniff into the pillow as the hot, salty sobs begin again.

"Aww… sweetie," my aunt says softly. "What's wrong?"

"Patrick and I had fight," I whimper.

Andi continues to rub my head much like my mom—my adopted mom—did when I was little and would fall down or crash my bike or any of the other myriad accidents I had. "People who love each other have arguments. That's life," Andi says. "I remember Andy telling me that he and Emily fussed over everything. It was how they were. But they loved fiercely and apparently, the making up was the fun part."

It's weird to hear stories about my *real* parents as actual people and not spirits. Not that I've met my dad on the other side. Still, to imagine them as living, breathing people who argued and loved… well, if makes me sad that I never got to know them or experience their love, even though I'm a product of it.

I twist and look up at her through the sheen of fresh water-works. "That's just it. I totally love him, but he's never said it to me. So, I don't know if he loves me or not."

"Of course he does. It's apparent to anyone who watches the two of you."

"Really?"

She nods her dark head. "Look, let him wallow in his boy world today. I'm taking you out on the town. Gather your girlfriends and let's go. The full London experience, on me."

I swipe my hand under my nose. "Fish and chips?"

"Of course. Although, London's more famous these days for its curry."

I screw up my nose a bit. "I think I'd rather have fish and chips."

Aunt Andi smacks me on the hip. "Up and at 'em. Both feet on the floor. This city was founded in 43 A.D. We've got a lot of history to check out."

❧ ❧ ❧

I've never had so much fun just... being.

Tears are long behind me and I'm enjoying hanging out with my gals. We set out on foot to see this amazing city via the Tube, the underground subway. Celia, Taylor, Maddie, Jessica, and Jayne are with us and it's a laugh a minute. We pop all over town to see the Tate Modern gallery—Gaugin's work in person is breathtaking—and take a ride on the London Eye. We also take in a walking tour of the House of Parliament, and then make our way through Westminster Abbey, marveling at the memorials of so many famous people like William Blake, all three Bronte sisters, Robert Burns, Lord Byron, Lewis Carroll, Chaucer, Churchill, holy crap... that's just the beginning of the alphabet. And even The Bard, himself, William Shakespeare. It's a life-sized white marble statue of him leaning on one elbow against a stack of books and manuscripts.

Celia is in awe. Total, complete wonder and admiration.

"Breath, Cel," I remind her.

She mimics his pose and I click away several pics of her. She does the same for me and then we join hands and giggle wildly. We may not make it to Stratford upon Avon to visit his actual grave, but this is the next best thing for Shakespearean geeks like the two of us.

While in the Abbey, I ignore the many spirits that are reaching out to me. I know they're there, calling to me and waving their celestial arms in my direction. I'm unsure as to whether they just want attention, acknowledgment, or help getting into the light. It's not that I'm unsympathetic to their plight; rather, I just want to be Kendall Moorehead. Teenager. Tourist.

"Oh, my," Taylor exclaims. "It's Sir Laurence Olivier!"

I suppose we all have our hero worshiping.

My hunger is satiated with a healthy serving of fish and chips near Piccadilly Circus, then we hop the Tube over to the Baker Street stop for a visit to Madam Tussauds. It's the cheesiest thing in the world: a room full of famous wax people. I have a blast, though, posing with the likenesses of Nicole Kidman, Leonardo DiCaprio, Lady Gaga, President Obama, and even the Queen herself. Okay, not really herself, but her wax self. Incredible! It's almost as good as meeting the real people... well, almost. I'm totally blowing up my Facebook with pictures of every single thing we're doing.

We round out our full day of touristy stuff by visiting the Tower of London. This place is amazing, with its steeped history as a city landmark, a refuge for royalty, a fortress, the home of the crown jewels, and the famed prison of so many of Henry VIII's political and religious rivals.

The seven of us pay our ticket price and make our way into the courtyard, past the beefeaters standing guard. The yard is full of enormous black crows milling about.

"You could put a saddle on that thing," Celia says, pointing at one near us.

Taylor squeals and backs away. "I hate birds."

Jayne reaches down and strokes the crow on its head. It's as though she and the bird are connected. "Poor bloke has had his wings clipped," she tells us. "They've done it for centuries so they won't fly off." I watch as she bonds with the creature. "He's happy here, though. He gets a lot to eat and the tourists take a lot of pictures of him."

I smile at her, and then she sort of snaps out of her trance.

"Sorry," she says.

"Don't be."

"That's how this whole thing started with me. I could hear the thoughts of the dogs and cats at home. Then I picked up on dead animal spirits."

My temple aches as Jayne talks. *A pounding out and an echoed scream from a time long ago. A female pleading for her life. Retching emotional pain ripped from her heart.* I hear her pleas, her begging, and her cries. I want to reach out to her, even though I don't know who she is. A spirit from a time long gone. Someone stuck in an eternal prison, or perhaps just residual memories from all the death this location has witnessed.

Jayne continues, "It's all so disturbing to hear these voices, spirits... the dead."

I know.

"Not at all," Jessica chimes in. "We all have our special gifts. You just have to learn what you're meant to do with yours."

Maybe so, but it doesn't make the psychic headache I'm experiencing any less knotty.

"Are you okay?" Aunt Andi asks.

I wince slightly. "We're not alone here. And I'm not talking about the other tourists."

"Oh, sweetie...."

Celia waves us over to an opening leading up to one of the towers. "Y'all check this out. I'm getting wicked spikes on my KII meter."

I laugh in spite of my discomfort. Only Celia Nichols would bring an EMT detector along to a tourist location. She's right, though. The lights are buried deep into the red zone. Spirits are around us.

Taylor reads from the brochure and map of the Tower. "It says that ghosts abound here. Follow me."

She leads us to an area known as the Haunted Gallery. Then she reads again from the tour brochure. "Catherine Howard, the fifth wife of King Henry VIII was accused in 1541 of adultery and put under house arrest here. She escaped, though, from her guards and ran down the gallery looking for the king to plead for her life. She was caught and dragged back screaming to her room and eventually executed at the Tower of London."

Well, that explains it. Poor Catherine. Poor Anne Boleyn for that matter and all of the other victims who died at the hands of Henry VIII. Their spiritual imprints are definitely still here. Locked in these walls. Recorded in the hallways and rooms.

Jayne says quietly, "There's so much going on here."

That's an understatement, I think, as I rub at the pain in my temple. Suddenly, my neck aches, burning hot and searing like I've gotten a nasty cut. I pull my hands up to my throat and realize I'm empathizing with the beheading victims. I try to breathe through the feelings, knowing it's not happening to me, but it's one of the most difficult things I've ever done.

The other girls have wandered off deeper into the gallery in search of the crown jewels room. Only Jayne remains with me. Perfectly still at my side.

"You feel it, don't you, Kendall." It's a statement from her, not a question.

"Yes," I eke out.

"Me too. They're scaring me."

"I know. They can't hurt you, though." I say this as if I believe it. I don't want to tell Jayne about the spirit back in Radisson that pushed me down the stairs, putting me in the hospital fighting for my life and having a near death experience. I want to think that was the exception and not the rule.

"I wish Christian were here. He'd know what to do," Jayne says.

"He's not the answer to everything," I tell her. "His ways and means are a little unorthodox."

Jayne seems shocked at my words. "Christian is *amazing*. My mother saw one of his gallery readings when he was up in Aberdeen. He picked up that I was having psychic flashes and offered to help me out. He's got the deepest eyes I've ever seen. He's gorgeous and perfect and can channel these spirits. And he's bloody brave to take on these evil spirits."

I continue to massage my head. "If you believe that's what he's doing."

"Why wouldn't I believe him? You've seen what's happened so far."

"I know, Jayne. Things might not be as they seem, though." I don't want to bust her chops, but I also don't want her world to spin around a Christian-only axis.

However, it may be too late.

Jayne's mouth drops open. "You don't understand, Kendall. Christian is a messenger of God. He's been told all his life that he has a mission to fulfill. That he has to defeat evil and fight these demons that are out to destroy him. Did you know his last three girl-friends tried to make him think he was crazy? They didn't believe him and did all these awful things to him. He said one of them had a nasty spiritual attachment. He tried to get a priest to bless her and she got all crazy and tried to kill him."

"That's a bit dramatic," I say, wondering how much of this is actually true. "Christian's not the only one who can help you out while you're discovering and exploring your gift, Jayne. I'm here for you, too."

"He's a prophet, Kendall. He says so and I believe him."

Now, more than ever, I'm convinced that Christian Campbell either has a screw loose or an agenda of some sort. I intend to get to the bottom of it and expose him for the fraud both Patrick and I believe him to be, if it comes to that.

Taylor calls out to me. "Kendall, you've got to come check out the bling!"

I follow down the hallway to find Taylor standing in awe in front of the amazing crown with the purple velvet lining underneath and white fur trim that I've seen Queen Elizabeth wearing when she opens Parliament.

Taylor gasps and puts her hands to her mouth. "*Mère de Dieu.* It has two thousand eight hundred and sixty-eight diamonds, two hundred seventy three pearls, seventeen sapphires, eleven emer-alds, and five rubies."

Celia harrumphs sarcastically. "Only five rubies? Wow."

I smack her on the arm. "Don't be rude."

She won't let up though, pointing at a round gold ornament, seeded with pearls and sapphires. "Look, an orb!"

Leave it to Celia to make me laugh when I'm being mentally tortured by spirits surrounding me—and worries of Christian Campbell and exactly what his glitch is. "It's the Sovereign's Orb," I say, correcting her.

"It's an orb, nonetheless," she quips. "See, not all orbs are made from dust particles, insects, or moisture in the air."

"Ever the ghost hunting investigator, eh Cel?"

She laughs at me. "I calls `em as I sees `em."

I'm about to replay my own witty comeback, when I'm suddenly struck with a lightning flash of psychic pain. Only this time, it's not from any of the residents of the Tower of London. It's a blazing bright warning that I can do nothing about. A silent threat to someone I love.

My hand slips up to my throat where I'm about to choke on the lump threatening to overtake me.

A soft voice whispers near me. A caution of what's to come.

It's not Anona. I don't know who this is, though, this new spirit guide or person that's watching over me. The voice is neither male nor female. It's filled with urgency.

Another flash. Blinding my sight.

The stench of terror fills my nostrils and I want to be sick.

Right here in front of the Queen's beautiful jewel collection.

Aunt Andi calls out to me, or maybe it's Celia. I can't tell.

I fall to my knees and clutch my heart that's ripping and burning with immense pressure.

For in my mind's eye, I see Patrick. He's somewhere in London. He's about to—

The scream rips involuntarily from my throat shaking me from head to toe.

Help him!

...and then I pass out cold.

CHAPTER TWELVE

When I finally come to, I'm back in my hotel room in bed with Aunt Andi sitting next to me. She presses a cold cloth to my head and smiles down at me.

"I think she's coming around."

I blink hard to focus well on my surroundings. Celia's sitting on the other side of me with a look of grave concern on her face.

"How did I get here?" I ask weakly.

"Believe it, or not," my aunt begins, "We got you into a cab and whisked you back. I was going to take you to the hospital, but Jayne and Maddie reached out to you and saw the panic in your head. I thought it best to get you some rest since you didn't sleep last night."

I twist to try and see the clock. "What time is it?"

Taylor's sitting nearby in a chair. Her usually tan skin is pale in the early evening light. "It's about six," she says.

"Wh-wh-what's wrong? Something's wrong!" I sit up too fast, getting a nasty head rush. Then the memories cascade back on me like a waterfall. "Oh, my God! Patrick!"

Aunt Andi shushes me and holds on to my shoulders. "There's been an accident. Patrick's at the hospital."

Tears burst from my eyes. "No!"

Celia takes my hand and holds on tightly. Why is this happening? What's going on?

Andi tries to calm me. "He's going to be okay."

"Really?" I ask through a sniff. "Tell me everything."

"The guys were touring Churchill's Cabinet War rooms. They came outside and Patrick claims that something pushed him from behind and literally propelled him out into traffic in front of an oncoming taxi," Andi says.

Something? Or *someone*. My worst fear threatens to overtake me, as I wonder if Jason had anything to do with it.

"You say he's okay?"

Andi nods and Celia takes over. "Jason called. I talked to him. He said Patrick's one 'in shape dude.' Seems he sort of jumped up onto the hood of the taxi and rolled off to the side. If he hadn't done that, he might have been hurt badly."

Okay, if Jason called to tell us, then maybe he wasn't involved. I certainly don't want to think that he'd be capable of injuring another person out of spite.

I lay back into the pillows and release a sigh. Closing my eyes, I try to reach out and connect psychically with Patrick. There's a blockage, though. Like a black curtain separating us and keeping us from each other. Where is this coming from? Patrick can't still be mad at me and pushing me away, can he?

Half an hour later, the guys return. I propel myself into Patrick's good arm—since the other is in a loose sling—for a tight hug with all my might. He doesn't push me away at all. In fact, he grips me firmly, nuzzling his face against my neck.

"Oh, Patrick, I knew something had happened. Someone whispered to me. I was so worried."

"Shhh... it's okay. I'm fine."

"No, you're not." I step away, not breaking contact. "You've got a sprained wrist and a broken rib."

He smiles brightly at me, his Hershey eyes sparkling. "What are you...psychic?"

I lift up on my tiptoes and kiss him smack on the lips. Nothing romantic. More like a desperate need to make sure I can still do this. He returns the kiss, sipping at my mouth in a way that tells me everything's more than okay between us.

He's here.

He's okay.

It could have been much, much worse.

Oliver breathes a sigh of relief. "There, there. I think that's enough excitement for one day. I'll order some pizza for everyone and we'll stay in and watch a movie. How does that sound?"

Patrick hugs me to him again, and I peer over his shoulder to find Jason watching us. At that moment, I see Jason's concern and concern over the situation. He sees the connection that Patrick and I have. I've never really witnessed someone's aura like Jessica can, but at that moment, I literally visualize the feelings Jason has for me... pop in the air and disappear. Snap, in fact. Like some weird effect from a cartoon, yet it's real. And it's okay. There's no hatred or hurt in his eyes. Just an understanding that we're over. An acceptance that Patrick and I are together.

Relief flows over me that Jason didn't have anything to do with Patrick's injury.

Then my gaze touches upon steely gray ones. Eyes that pierce my soul with a sinister sneer.

To be an alleged "messenger of God," Christian Campbell certainly seems like the devil himself.

I'm not taking my eyes off this creep.

⚜   ⚜   ⚜

The next day, Oliver's set up a special banquet room for us at the Bag `O Nails pub—for a traditional roast beef and Yorkshire pudding meal—and then a tour of the public rooms at Buckingham Palace. He's really going all out for us with the red carpet treatment.

I also pick up from him that he's giving this full court press as a way to assuage some of what's gone wrong during this trip—the frustration from investigations gone badly as well as Patrick's accident.

However, the minute we leave the hotel to board our bus, we are swarmed by reporters and photographers. Ahh... the infamous paparazzi and London tabloid press here to photograph the American TV psychic and his....

Wait a second! They're all congregating around Christian?

"Christian! Christian, over here!" one photographer shouts out.

A reporter shoves a microphone in front of him. "You're the talk of London, Christian, can you give us a quote?"

"Tell us about the demonic entity you've been in contact with," another says.

"What is this 'Dojo Disturbance'?"

I whisper to Patrick, "How do these reporters know about Dojo enough to call him a disturbance?"

Patrick snickers. "Looks like good old Christian has been sending out press releases. I saw him on the computer a few nights ago on a newswire site. I should have put two and two together."

Everyone seems as shocked and surprised as I am to see the press flocking around our colleague. I look to Oliver to take control here, but he's standing tall next to the press's flavor of the moment, encouraging him and pushing him toward the cameras.

"Are you kidding me?" Sarcasm laces my voice.

Celia clicks her tongue. "You're not honestly surprised by this, I hope."

Christian preens for the reporters, smiling some, and looking off pensively at other moments. What a poser. Literally. And there's Oliver, the enabler. Great. Just great. Not that I want the attention or press. This isn't what this tour was supposed to be about. But I guess it is now.

Patrick wraps his good arm around me and pulls me close to him. His silent message is for me to keep my mouth shut and just smile. So I do.

"Mr. Campbell, tell us how you first connected with this Dojo entity," a female reporter asks in a thick Cockney accent.

Christian's face grows serious and he musters up some good acting for the cameras. "I've been haunted my whole life by this creature. Since I was a child of three and he stood at the end of my bed. I knew then that God had a special purpose for me. To be his messenger and to help defeat these demons roaming the earth."

I can't help but roll my eyes. Again with the prophet of God shtick.

"Dojo is a serious threat," Christian says. "It is my mission in life to reach out to as many people as possible who've been affected by this demon, to help them connect with their loved ones, and to push this entity into the underworld realm where he belongs."

The Cockney woman speaks up again. "Mr. Campbell, there are reports all over the Internet from people throughout the EU claiming to have been contacted by an entity named Dojo. People in London, Paris, Rome. What is your advice to them?"

Christian nods his perfectly coifed head. "It's very simple. They need to contact me. I am the only person—sent by God—who can defeat this monster."

I can't take this anymore. "Give me a break."

I spin on my heels and bolt back into the hotel lobby. Patrick, Celia, and Jason follow suit.

"This is complete crap," I say to them once we're inside.

Outside, I can see the camera flashes highlighting Christian in all his glory. They're eating up his every word. Charm oozes from his every orifice. Oliver turns and sees that we've fled back into the hotel, and he steps in to join us.

Before I can speak, Patrick snaps out, "Oliver, what the hell is going on here?"

I point. "That's a joke out there. This isn't what I signed up for this summer."

Only Jayne remains outside with Christian and his audience, as Jessica, Maddie and Taylor join us in the lobby.

Oliver gathers us around and fends off my verbal attack by holding up his arms. "I had originally formed this trip for my top students so you could help me with some important cases I'd been asked about and to help continue your psychic development." He pauses for effect. Or possibly as a delay tactic. "However, word has gotten out—mainly through my own show producers—about Christian, his abilities, and his growing popularity here in the UK. They want to follow him around and focus on his plight with this Dojo entity and the connection Christian has with it."

Jessica shakes her head, her red hair nearly blazing with her own intense aura. "You've got to be kidding me, Oliver. That kid is whack."

"Now, Jessica—"

"No, seriously. His aura is mucked up like nobody's business," she snaps. "I can't believe someone with your reputation and strong moral character would fall for whatever he's peddling."

Oliver frowns at my friend and roommate. "Jealousy is a nasty thing, Jessica."

"I'm so totally not jealous of him," she says. Her face falls and I can see the pain and confusion emanating off her. Disgust steams off her skin and I'm saddened because I know what she's going to say next. "I think I need to go home."

"Jess, no," I plead.

She holds her hand up. "No, Kendall, it's okay. I'm really grossed out by this. Something's just not right. You know it. We all know it." She glares at Oliver. "Most of us know it, that is."

Oliver crosses his arms over his chest. "Jessica, I think you're acting very childishly. I handpicked you for this journey and you're being quite ungrateful."

She hangs her head. "I'd like to go home, please. You owe me that."

"Fine," Oliver says. "I'll have my assistant arrange it."

This totally sucks. I'm losing my roommate all because of some overly polished pretty boy who thinks he's the next big TV psychic. It's bad enough that every paranormal group in America is filming a pilot, hoping to be picked up by whatever cable channel. Now, we have to kowtow to this...this...fraud? This isn't fair at all, yet I know I can't leave. I have to stay and make sure this piece of human excrement doesn't get away with this, or worse, hurt any-one—including himself or Jayne—in the process.

Maddie, the empath, begins to cry. Not in a babyish way, rather in a sympathetic manner to Jessica's pain and what the rest of us are feeling. "I'd like to leave, too." She wipes away the tears from underneath her eyes.

"Not you, too, Maddie," Oliver pleads.

"I can't handle all these emotions I'm getting," she says. "This one is jealous. That one's confused. Another one is cocky and self-assured and none of us are here for the right reasons anymore."

Tension sets in Oliver's jaw as he glares at my friends. "I can't tell you how disappointed I am in you, as well."

Maddie shrugs. "I'm just a country girl from Alabama, Oliver. I miss my sisters. Both of them were against my coming on this trip. I should have listened to them. I'll fly back to the states with Jessica, please."

Impertinent, Oliver stands tall and stares out. "I don't want anyone doing anything that makes them uncomfortable. I'm sad to see you both go, but we'll just have to carry on with the rest of our tour."

Jessica reaches for Maddie's hand and together the two of them head toward the lift to go to our room and pack.

Oliver levels his eyes directly at me. "We have more investigations to conduct. People who need our help. That is if no one else is bailing." He lifts an inquisitive brow at me, but he already knows the answer. He is one of the world's top psychics, after all.

I look at my team—Celia, Taylor, Patrick, and Jason—and they all nod back at me. We know what we have to do. There's very obviously something dark that we're working against and we have to see things through. No matter how much it pains me, I know we're in this for the duration of the summer, even if it is in the shadow of Christian Campbell's limelight.

Speaking for the five of us, I say, "You can count on us."

Oliver smiles. "Very well. Let's get back to work."

CHAPTER THIRTEEN

Talk about feeling inadequate and unnecessary.

The rest of our time in London is nothing but The Christian Campbell Show. All day. Every day.

It's not that I need to be the center of attention. Not at all. But I would like to feel useful and that's just not the case now that Oliver has shifted the focus of our summer tour to promoting Christian and getting him as much press as possible.

Right now, I'm sitting next to Patrick in the front row of the audience of at least a hundred and fifty people here at London's Bridewell Theatre. Christian is performing a gallery reading to suckers, err, I mean people who paid fifty euros each to see if one of their relatives or deceased loved ones comes through to the teen psychic who's been all over the news, tabloids, and newspapers. I even had a comment on my Facebook page from Courtney Langdon back home totally freaking out that I know Christian Campbell and can I get his autograph for her.

Umm, no.

According to The London Mirror, the Scottish Clairvoyant has "taken the world by storm" and now people are coming out of the woodwork—ha, get it...Ouija boards are made of wood—saying they, too, have heard from an entity named Dojo.

I just don't buy it.

But here I sit. Participating. Smiling. Supporting. Listening.

Christian, wearing a black silk shirt opened a little bit too much at the neck and a pair of two hundred dollar jeans, paces in front of the audience with his fingers tented together.

"I should have slept in today," Jason mutters from behind me. "This is craptastic."

I shush him, although I agree whole-heartedly.

Christian points to the end of the second row where an elderly woman sits with a walker propped next to her. She's clutching her rosaries. "I'm sensing someone right here with health issues."

Jason and Celia chortle at the same time and I cough to cover their guffaw.

"What was his first clue?" Jason whispers. "Couldn't have been her crutch."

"I'm getting an M name, attached to a B name. Anyone?"

Six hands go up, including the elderly lady. "My name is Mary and my husband was Bernard." She pronounces it like "burn-erd."

Okay, an M name attached to a B name... Mary and Bernard. I'll give him that one. Sort of.

He approaches her closely, nodding. "Bernard is on the other side, isn't he?"

She gasps and bobs her head.

"And he was strong in his Catholic faith."

Again, a yes.

Christian kneels next to her. "I'm sensing a circulatory issue in your legs, Mary. Bernard wants you to make sure you listen to your doctors and do as they say."

She sniffles. "Yes, yes..."

"And he stresses to me that he's in a good place and he's very happy."

Tears fill Mary's eyes and I want to go smack Christian for manipulating this woman. He stares down at her shirt and I notice what he's obviously seeing. She's covered in cat hair all over her black blouse.

"He's mentioning a family pet," Christian says. "A pussy cat."

"Yes! Mr. Sparkles," Mary exclaims.

"He's really good," Taylor says to me.

"Get real. He's nothing but a fake."

Has she not been paying attention? One doesn't have to be a nuclear physicist to see that Christian Campbell is a cold reader.

He observes, he processes, and he uses the information to his advantage.

To Patrick, I say, *I've never seen a bigger fraud in my life.*

A fraud who Oliver supports.

What can we do?

Nothing. Yet. He'll fall on his own sword soon enough.

But when? In the meantime, all of these people are paying good money to hear him tell them things they already know.

There's more to it, Patrick says in my head.

What?

He has a darkness around him. A low lying black density that surrounds him.

Jessica saw it.

And that's why she left.

What can we do?

Watch him. Closely.

Great. In the meantime, the little shit gets seventy-five hundred pounds for today's performance.

Not a bad take.

And Oliver believes in this kid to the detriment of the rest of our group. We sit here like mere fans, pawns in the psychic chess match. I don't need to be photographed or interviewed, but I have abilities and see things others don't.

Like Princess Di who is here in the audience. She's standing toward the back in a white sleeveless dress. Her hair is brushed away from her face and she clutches a small purse. Odd that she's just hanging back like that. I wave to her and she signals to me. I wonder if she's here to connect with someone or if she's just curious about Christian.

Patrick elbows me and I jump a bit. "Listen to what's going on."

I turn my attention back to Christian and the thirty-something man he's now reading. A glance behind me, and I see that the princess is no longer there. I shrug inwardly; still curious as to why she's hanging around us... around me.

"Oh, my," Taylor says through hissed teeth. "Is that what I think it is?"

"I brought this with me today," the man says to Christian and hands him the polished board.

"Another Ouija board," Celia notes.

"We're going to need a whole other bedroom just for his collection," Jason quips.

"Tell me where you got this, sir," Christian presses.

"My grandmother bought it in Germany in the 1970s. It's been in our family ever since. We've used it at parties and such as a conversational piece. Lately, though, it's been calling to me and I've gotten the same name over and over again."

"Really now? Let me see."

Christian sits and places his hands on the planchette. I don't have to be psychic to know what's coming next. Closing his eyes, he begins to rock back and forth a bit. "There is a spirit attached to this board. Come forth and speak to us."

The audience leans forward in unison to watch. I let out a long sigh.

"Speak to me," Christian demands. "Tell me your name."

The planchette moves around on the board and the man who brought it calls out what it spells. "D. O. J. O. I'll be damned if that isn't the name I've been getting as well."

"Isn't that convenient," I say, slumping in my seat.

But just as my doubts are solidifying in a not-so-positive opinion of Christian Campbell, I see exactly what Patrick is talking about. A dark black mist hovers near Christian's feet, circling and swirling around him, encompassing him in a twirl of negativity. He's so caught up with what he's doing and so in love with the sound of his own voice, that I don't think he realizes this *entity* or attachment is there.

Does he even see it?

I don't think so. Because as Christian hands the Ouija board back to the man and then bows when the audience begins its standing ovation, this darkness stands up right next to him, wrapping malevolent tentacles around the young guy.

Right then, my eyes sync with the being—if it even is a being— and I hear a deep, guttural hissing sound like a snake saying, "He is miiiiiiiiiiiine."

Holy shit.

Is this Dojo thing for real?

❧ ❧ ❧

"Kendall, hurry up!" Celia shouts at me. "We're going to miss the train if you don't put the moves on."

Our time in London is over and we're taking the Eurorail through the Chunnel tonight over to Paris. While I itch with excitement to get to the City of Love and see Becca in her DJ contest, I'm leaving England's capitol with an extremely sour taste in my mouth.

Christian collected four Ouija boards in our time here, each one of them spelling out the name "Dojo" to audiences small and large. He's been courted by the press and made the front page news with his "Dojo Disturbance." Yet, he doesn't seem to get that he's either delving into dark magic or opening up a portal to a realm he has no idea how to deal with. If it is all just bull honkus—which I still think it is—there are kids like Jayne who are using Christian as a role model and that's a dangerous spiral to wind down.

"Kendall!" This time it's Taylor calling out. "We've got to go!"

"Okay, okay!" I shove the last of my toiletries into my makeup bag and cram it into my suitcase. The stupid thing won't shut so I have to sit on top of it to smash everything down.

Aunt Andi pops her head in. "It's now or never, babe."

Reluctantly, I leave my lovely London home, yet look forward to a new adventure ahead. With all that's happened in this city, I feel like our work is left… undone. So many questions left unanswered, yet Oliver seems content enough to move us along. I thought we were here to help people with hauntings in their homes and connecting with their loved ones. However, all of this just got tossed out the window once Christian Campbell moved center stage into the main spotlight. And what of Princess Di? Have I seen the last of her?

There's an inkling inside of me that Christian is going to get what's coming to him. That karma's going to catch up and kick him squarely in the behind. I don't wish it on him; I just know it's going to happen.

Everyone's gathered down in the lobby and Oliver rallies us toward the double-decker bus one last time. Swiftly, our ride delivers us to the train station where we board the Eurorail for the two-hour journey to Paris.

Taylor sits next to me on the bus, not even thinking that I might want to sit with Patrick. He's got his headphones and sunglasses on, though, so it's okay.

"I can't believe I'm going to Paris," my friend says. "I've wanted to visit Paris my entire life."

I snicker. "You're only seventeen."

"I know, but still. The Seine, the Champs-Élysées, the Louvre, ahhhh…"

From the look in Taylor's eyes, I see the distant love for a city and a culture she worships. I'm so glad she could come along this summer, even though it's turned out to be a different experience than I'd expected.

We arrive at St. Pancras station in London just in time to board the train headed to Paris's Gard du Nord. Or North Station as Taylor, Little Miss French, tells me.

Although I thought everything was good between Patrick and me, he still seems a little distant.

"Are we okay?" I ask.

Patrick plays with the train ticket in his hand. "Yeah, I suppose."

I lay my hand on his arm, hoping to connect more with him. He stops and looks down at where I'm touching him. His usual warm smile that comes from our closeness isn't there. Instead, I read so much pain, confusion, and worry on his handsome face. "Something's bothering you."

He flattens his mouth. "Understatement of the year, Kendall."

I move my hand onto my hip. "Honestly, you're not still miffed about Jason, are you? I told you that—"

Patrick waves me off like an annoying fly. "I don't care about Tillson. Whatever. He's harmless. I'm worried about *him*." He points ahead at Christian, who's signing an autograph for a lady who's cooing all over him. "He's brought a darkness to our group. I'm watching him like a hawk."

"Are you going to sit with me on the train?" I'd hoped for a little cuddly-snuggle time during the blacked-out Chunnel portion of the trip, which takes us under the Strait of Dover over to France.

He rubs his eyes with the index finger and thumb on his non-sprained hand. "Maybe. I don't know. I've got a lot on my mind, Kendall."

Like he's the only one. I'm tired of trying to spark the romance on this trip. "Fine. Be that way." Stupid boy.

I spin away from him and catch up with Celia and Jason who are already boarding the train.

"Don't be like that," Patrick calls out. "Kendall!"

It's too late. If he's going to put distance between us, then let him. He's not the only one concerned about Mr. Campbell. But I'm not going to let it ruin the most romantic city on planet earth. Patrick can pout and be pensive on the ride over. However, once we're in France, he better man up on the passion part.

Inside the train, I find Jayne seated alone, staring out the window.

"May I sit with you?"

She bobs her head; a pout crosses her face.

"What's wrong?

"Christian's all but ignoring me. He's got the press around him and he's loving the attention. He's forgotten about me."

I stow my suitcase overhead and then rest my backpack on the seat next to me, facing my friend. "He's a guy. They thrive on attention."

"How am I supposed to learn things from him when he's so busy fighting Dojo?"

"That's what you've got me for," I say with a wide smile.

Celia, Jason, and Taylor take the next compartment over, and I see that Patrick's opted for a seat on his own. As the train lumbers away from England and out underneath the English Channel, I lay my head back and try to relax as the car rocks softly back and forth with a chugging rhythm.

I'm not sure how long I've been asleep or whether I'm actually dreaming when I sit up and feel a chilling draft in the compartment. Jayne's spread out on her seat, sound asleep, her glasses askew on her face. The air density in our area thickens and I find it a bit hard to intake a strong breath. My chest feels tight and heavy as though something is sitting on me.

Then, a misshaped figure much like a see-through black specter takes form and begins to hover over Jayne. Fingers of curiosity stretch out at her, and I feel like I'm trapped in a *Harry Potter* novel watching the Dementors begin to suck the life out of people.

"Leave her alone," I shout.

The figure freezes and then zings out of the cabin. A chilling cold follows in its waking, bringing chill bumps dancing all up and down my arms as though I've gone outside in December without my coat on. Only, it's the dead of summer.

"What the—"

Anona materializes next to me. Her beautiful face is drawn and concerned. "You have to protect her, Kendall."

"I'm trying. It's hard, though, when she has such hero-worship for Christian."

"She's young and confused. She looks up to you," my spirit guide tells me.

"I know. I told her I'm here for her." I grasp onto my train seat as the car rocks back and forth on the rails. It's as though it's trying to shake off the evil presence that's traveling along with us from the British Isles over to France.

Anona, unaffected by the motion, says, "You must do more. There are dark forces at play, Kendall."

I lean forward. "Like what?"

Her voice echoes out around me. "Everything is not as it appears."

"You keep telling me that, Anona." I want to pull my hair out of my head. "Why can't you be more specific? I can't fight something if I don't know exactly what I'm up against."

"I've done what I can, Kendall. Watch over Jayne. I can go no farther with you."

"Anona, please! You can't leave me."

"You're not alone. You're never alone."

She fades away, though. Gone, as quickly as she arrived. The details of her face melt away into a thin fog that quickly dissipates. The temperature of the compartment returns to normal, almost stifling now as I try to breath through the warning Anona tossed out at me. The car lists to the left as we're, no doubt, going around a curve, and I hold on, letting Anona's words sink in. Frustration courses through my veins as fast as this train zipping over the rails.

I slam my fist to the seat and pound the fabric a few times in utter frustration.

I watch Jayne sleeping, vulnerable and so naïve.

And I've never felt so alone in my whole life.

CHAPTER FOURTEEN

I slip out of the train compartment and down the corridor to the washroom. I splash water on my face, letting the frigid liquid wake me out of my shockwave of disbelief. I slide my hands over my cheeks and try to shake off everything. Anona's warning. The specter over Jayne. The mistrust of Christian. The confusion over the way this trip is turning out.

When I leave the washroom, I peak in on Patrick, hoping to tell him what happened. He's spread out on his seat, asleep with his sunglasses in place and his headphones spilling out Dance music in a blaring tone. Instead of waking him, I bend down and kiss him on the cheek, smoothing a lock of his thick hair to the side.

My stomach growls out its discomfort, so I head off to find the food car to see what they have to offer. Holding on to the hallway railings as the train rocks from side to side, I queue up behind a French couple and then order a croissant and a Coke Light. (I love the European name for my beloved Diet Coke.) After I hand over a couple of euros, I make my way into the club car and see Christian sitting in a booth with his laptop open in front of him.

"Well, look who's up," I say, trying to steal a glance at his screen.

He quickly snaps the lid shut and places his hands on top of the computer. Even my intense psychic abilities can't penetrate the casing of his machine to see what he's up to. Probably doing an Excel spreadsheet for all of the bank he made in London.

"Miss Moorehead," he says formally.

I smirk at him. "I'm not calling you Mr. Campbell, Christian."

"I was merely being polite." He motions across from him. "Please, join me."

Reluctantly, I slide into the seat and set my drink and food in front of me. I pinch off the end of the croissant and pop the buttery pastry into my mouth.

Christian leans forward, his gray eyes penetrating me. "I know all about you, Miss Moorehead."

"Kendall," I say after I swallow. "My name is Kendall. We're like seventeen, not fifty, Christian."

"As you please," he says. His hands rest on the top of his computer and for the first time, I notice the rings he has on. One is a silver cross and the other appears to be some sort of onyx devil head. An odd choice for someone who claims to be a messenger of God.

Finally, he breaks the awkward silence. "You're searching for answers."

Yeah... solutions for what this kid is really up to. I lift my eyes to his, but don't let on anything. "Aren't we all?"

Christian waggles his index finger at me, gray eyes slanted as he's obviously trying to read me. "Your father. He's a wandering soul."

I drop my gaze from his and pick at the croissant. "You don't know that. My dad is a city planner back in Georgia. The only wandering he does is around the town."

He shakes his head at me. "No, Kendall. Your father will know no peace until you complete your journey."

Okay, I mostly think this kid is a top-shelf fake and a fraud, but how does he purport to know about my father. Unless he's talking about... Andy?

Christian raises a brow. "Yes. Your *birth* father."

"Stop it," I say firmly. "You don't impress me."

He slicks his hand through his salon-perfect highlighted hair, making it stand on end even more. "Why not?"

I want to reach over and mess it up more than anything. Instead, I fix my stare at him and calmly say, "I'm not one of your fans."

He levels his eyes at me again. "No, you're not, are you?"

I want to shirk off his words, but inwardly, I'm shaking something fierce. For all I know, Patrick, Jason, or Aunt Andi—anyone—could have shared my backstory with Christian. It's not exactly a secret that I'm adopted, after all. Anger seethes through me at the thought of this guy trying to manipulate me by touching on my weak point.

"Tread lightly with me, Christian," I say in a bit of a laced warning.

"You know, Kendall," Christian says. "We're cut from the same cloth, you and me. We both have a purpose in life."

After chewing another bite of my snack, I say, "Everyone has a purpose in life. That's why we're all here."

Another shake of the head as Christian scoffs. "Our abilities are special. We can do things others can't. We are prophets on this earth, sent to do God's work. People will pay for our services to seek out answers, guidance, and solutions for their problems."

I flatten my lips. "Last I checked, prophets don't feel the need to make a profit."

He gives me a boy shrug, dismissing my comment like it's a pestering fly. "The things I've seen. The experiences I've had. Nothing will stop me on my mission."

"What exactly is that?" I grab my soda and quench my parched throat.

"People have tried to keep me from what I a supposed to be doing. My mother. My Anglican priest. My girlfriends, particularly. Every one I've had a significant relationship with has tried to destroy me and keep me from my undertaking. They're out to annihilate me by allowing Dojo to possess them. He's trying to take my trust and ability to love away from me."

"Dojo's taking your love," I repeat a bit sarcastically. See, I don't exactly believe that this *thing* has been haunting him since he was a wee lad.

Christian's eyes widen. "After I broke up with Mary McDonahue last month, she was met at the front stoop of my house by a handsome, dark man in an expensive suit. He curled his lip and said to her, 'Good work,' and then he just disappeared."

Too bad I can't text this Mary McDonahue to get her own version of this encounter. Something tells me it would be quite different.

Instead, I say, "You assume this handsome dark man was Dojo."

"I do *not* assume," he snaps. "He seeks my obliteration."

And here I thought *I* had boy problems. My love triangle is nothing compared to Christian's messed-up view of relationships. He's either completely full of shit and just upping his game to get a television show and more people at his psychic galleries, or he's so narcissistic that he wouldn't be able to see reality if it sat in his lap. I slurp at my soda and shake my head at the creative fiction Christian Campbell is weaving before me.

"You know what? You need to lighten up," I say. "You're way too intense and need to just chillax and be a teenager. Get a girlfriend. Go to the movies. Read a book. Get obsessed with Farmville or something."

Christian actually softens and chuckles at me. Then he reaches out and grabs my hand. He tightens his grip while his thumb starts getting all caress-y on me. Sure, the guy is model gorgeous and most girls might swoon and fall into a gooey puddle at his feet, but I'm not most girls. He's getting too familiar with me, and that creeps me the hell out.

"I like you, Kendall," Christian says with a soft voice, almost attempting to hypnotize. "You might be the one to save me and help me believe in love again."

The intensity in his eyes has me pinned in place. Only momentarily, though. Compliments aside, I don't trust this guy.

Just as I'm about to pull my hand from his, I look up to find Patrick standing in the doorway of the club car with a soda in his hand. His mouth hangs open and his eyes speak of deep, layered disappointment.

His lips don't move as he talks to me in my head.

First Tillson and now this tool?

It's not what you think, Patrick!

It's exactly what I think. He's holding your hand and professing his love to you.

No, he's not! Gross!

How am I supposed to keep trusting you, Kendall?

This guy is a lying snake!

And you're holding his hand.

Patrick spins on his heels and heads out of the car.

"Dammit!"

I jerk my hand away from Christian and rise to go after Patrick.

But not before I see the satisfied smirk on Christian's face.

CHAPTER FIFTEEN

I should be off my rocker with excitement as our train pulls into Gard du Nord in Paris. Ahh... the City of Love. However, I've spent the last hour trying to reassure Patrick that I'm crazy about *him* and not Jason Tillson. And certainly not that pompous narcissistic ass-hat, Christian Campbell.

"Look, Kendall," Patrick says as he hitches his backpack onto his shoulder. "Something's trying to wedge itself between us. It's trying to pull us apart."

"Then we can't let it."

His eyes intensify. "I can't fight something when I don't know what *it* is. A feeling? A premonition? A person? A demon? Campbell? Tillson's feelings for you? Is it something dark swirling around us? I don't know!"

"You think it's Dojo, don't you?"

Exasperated, Patrick throws his good hand up to his side. "I'm not convinced that Dojo actually exists."

I guess if we did think this demon was real, we wouldn't keep acknowledging it by saying the name out loud.

I grasp Patrick's hand and lace my fingers through his. I concentrate on spreading as much love from deep inside me to flow from my hands to his. Saying the words right now might be trite or desperate, but I do love him. So much. We're the same person. Meant to be together.

We're meant to be together.

He must hear me because he leans his forehead to meet up with mine. We stand like this for a moment—for an eternity—until

100

Patrick pulls back. But not away. He lowers his head and gently places his lips on mine for a sweet, sweet kiss. One that touches my toes and my soul at the same time. One that promises more. One that speaks of understanding and forgiveness.

I kiss him back, moving my lips against his in a heated sensation that makes me wish the rest of the world would disappear, and Patrick and I could fade into the beauty and background of this treasured city. For just a moment.

He does pull back this time, but a smile crosses his handsome face. "I'm sorry I've been so quick to judge you and everything that's going on."

I chuckle. "Yeah, that sucks, but then again, you're just a guy. What am I going to do with you?"

We laugh together and he shakes his head at me like "there Kendall goes again." Then he gets serious. We're going to make time for us," he says. "Patrick and Kendall time. Away from Christian and his sideshow and Oliver's plans for us."

I let out a sigh of relief knowing that things are going to be okay with us, despite Christian's manipulative attempt to come between us.

Speaking of the devil, Christian steps off the train and glares at me before sliding his sunglasses over his eyes. Jayne is by his side, trying desperately to regain his attention.

Oliver walks up and smiles brightly at us. "Well, I've massaged the phone lines and my contacts here in Paris and I'm thrilled to say I have a gallery reading set up for Christian at none other than the Ritz Carlton." Oliver twists the end of his mustache, quite pleased with himself.

Celia slips behind me. "Great," she whispers, "now he can scam the French out of their hard-earned money."

"I'm bored with this whole scene," Jason says. "We're in Paris, dude. Let's ditch this."

Celia smirks at him. "I have my AmEx."

"I have my PayPal savings," he says to her.

Taylor pouts and I feel her disappointment. She's in the place she's dreamed of and I intend to make sure my friend has the time of her life. Besides, Becca's counting on us to come to her DJ contest. It's time we break out on our own.

"I say we put the 'vacate' in 'vacation.'"

My friends agree and smile at me.

I'm tired of being a sidekick to this circus act. I have my own money, and I don't need to follow Oliver through this one-way trek. I look over at my aunt, who must have morphed into a psychic herself because I can tell she's reading my mind, or maybe she just sees my obvious exhaustion at the Christian Campbell dog and pony show.

"I'll take care of everything," Aunt Andi says, reaching for her cellphone.

I love that we understand each other on a much deeper level.

Christian clears his throat, and both he and Oliver look over at us.

"Something's wrong," Oliver states.

"Hello, Captain Obvious," Jason quips.

I step forward to speak for our group. "We're going to take a little break, Oliver. We need some time, umm, on our own. You and Christian have your focus that doesn't really include us, so we're going to hang out together for a few days."

Oliver crinkles his brow. "Kendall, that's not neces—"

"—yeah, it sort of is."

"She's right." Patrick places a hand on the small of my back.

Aunt Andi joins in. "I'll keep a watchful eye over them, Oliver. They won't be penniless, wandering the streets of Paris. I have some connections here and I've already set a plan in motion."

"If that's what you want," Oliver says.

"I think it's what's best," I tell him. Honestly, the guy is wicked psychic, yet he can't see that putting all of his metaphysical eggs in one basket with Christian has literally run off everyone from his summer tour. Maddie and Jessica wanting nothing to do with this and now we want to get away. I don't understand Oliver's blind faith in this kid.

Then there's Jayne. My heart aches as I glance over at the disappointment on her face. I'd promised Anona that I'd take care of the girl, yet here I am walking away from Christian's shenanigans.

GHOST HUNTRESS: THE JOURNEY

"You wanna come with us?" I ask her. I mean, I know her nice Scottish parents set her off on a chaperoned trip with the world-famous Oliver Bates, but I wish I could break her away from this idolized view of Christian and how he can "mentor" her.

She's thinking about it. I can see the gears churning in her head. But she pouts and shifts her eyes over to where Oliver is speaking with Christian. "I'm supposed to be learning from him."

"I understand." I don't really. "Do what you have to do. I just wanted you to know you're welcome to come with us." For me to protect you.

"I need to stay with Christian." Then Jayne adds with a bit of desperation in her voice, "You're coming back, right?"

"We're only going to be gone a couple of days," I tell her.

Aunt Andi rounds us up and we wave goodbye to Oliver, Christian, and Jayne. It's the right thing to do. We need a break. I need a break. I need time to think. To focus. To figure out what's going on here.

Celia takes my arm in hers. "Andi says this hotel has wi-fi, so I'm going to do some intense research on this kid and what he's up to."

I smile at my friend. "When did *you* become psychic?"

"When this douchebag came into our lives," she says with a laugh.

Jason and Patrick tend to all of our bags and load them into the cabs that we take over to the seventh arrondissment – whatever that means. I wish I'd spent more time researching the culture and language. I figured I'd be so busy with investigations and trying to help people with their own hauntings and such that I wouldn't have time to be a tourist. Christian's antics have changed everything.

"Arrondissments are districts," Taylor explains. "The city is broken up into different sections. The seventh is near the Eiffel Tower on the left bank of the Seine River. Very chic address. Prestigious area."

Ahhh...the Eiffel Tower. I can't wait to see that. That's the ultimate symbol of the city... and of love. I envision standing at the top with Patrick overlooking the Paris all lit up at night. We're hugged together and I feel at peace and so loved. Is this a vision, a memory, or a glance into the future?

Our cab lets us off on Rue Cler, a market street hustling and bustling with people rushing about between the stores. There's a butcher shop with hanging slabs of beef and pork in the window. Or is that horse meat? Eww! A patisserie, or bakery, has its doors wide open so that the sweet aroma of butter and chocolate tickle our noses. Another sign reads "boulangerie" and sports baguettes, rounds of bread, and other baked goods. Flowers in every color of the rainbow line the outside of another store, with a crepe vendor standing nearby, flipping over the thin pancakes for a hungry customer. A cheese shop nearby smells of the pungent scent of its wares. I cringe a bit at the sharp odor.

Taylor grins wide. "Fromageries in Paris are known for their stinkiness."

I want to laugh and gag all at the same time. "I think I'll stick to cheddar, thanks."

Celia stares up at the name of where we're going to stay. "Grand Hotel Leveque. Looks quaint."

Taylor breaks into a stream of French that I don't even try to interpret. She's in her element, flirting with a man who's holding the hotel door open for us.

"How did you find this place?" I ask my aunt.

"I stayed here when I was in college and did my backpacking thing. Back when their money was a franc instead of a euro. It's small, very European, but good for our purposes."

I hug her to me. "Thanks for making this happen."

"You needed a break, sweetie. I don't need psychic powers to see that you kids were not only being upstaged, but minimalized."

The lift—elevator—to the third floor barely holds two people. Celia blushes as Jason hops in with her and wraps his arms around her so they'll both fit. I wait for the jealousy to kick in, but it's not there. I'm okay with the fact that I'm not with Jason. And he's being civil and keeping his distance, respecting that I'm with Patrick.

Aunt Andi's and my room is at the front of the hotel with two small single beds. The décor is orange and brown, and we have a tiny wrought iron balcony that looks over Rue Cler. Celia and Taylor take the room next door and a third room across the hall is for the guys.

Jason pulls up short and looks at Patrick. "So, we're sharing?"

"Looks that way," Patrick says. "Don't worry, I don't snore that loudly."

Jason dashes a glance at me. "That's going to be a bit awkward, don't you think?"

"Why?" I chime in.

"Never mind," he mumbles.

Celia steps between them. "Get over it. We're only going to be sleeping and showering here. You boys won't have time to gossip about your love of Kendall."

Whoa! Celia Nichols! WTH!

Jason and Patrick back down from the argument and disappear into their room without another comment. Oh, man, to be a fly on *that* wall.

"Celia! Why did you say that?"

"*Elle est une lapalissade*," Taylor says.

"Huh? English, please."

Taylor smirks at me. "She's being honest."

"About what?"

"What?" Celia asks incredulously. "Like we don't all know what's going on here, Kendall."

Embarrassed beyond belief, I feel my face heat like a homecoming bonfire. Celia flattens her lips and places her hands on her hips. "Every guy on this trip is drooling over you, Kendall. You've got Patrick, that's true, but why do you think Jason is here, as well?"

"To protect Taylor."

"That's just an excuse," Taylor says. "He's here to be near you."

He did admit his feelings to me back in London, but I hadn't shared that little tidbit with anyone. I guess my friends are psychic, as well.

"Christian's got his sights on you, as well." Celia rocks back and forth on her feet. She's been unusually reserved so far on the trip, but she has something to say.

I click my tongue. "Christian's a troublemaker. And a real dick."

Celia shrugs. "Maybe. Still...."

I sigh hard. "Stop it! I don't want any of this. I just want to be with Patrick. He's the only one."

Celia hangs her head and then Taylor takes my hand gently in hers, very motherly, almost. "Then you need to tell it to Jason straight up. Once and for all."

I swallow hard. "Yeah, I guess I do."

⚜ ⚜ ⚜

A little while later, I find Jason out on Rue Cler in front of the flower shop. Or Cler Fleurs, as it's called in French. He's picking through pails of yellow daisies, white roses, and pink tulips that line the outside of the storefront stacked three deep. The sweet aromas of the many blossoms reach out and tickle my nose as I approach closer.

"Whatcha doing?" I ask, surprising him.

"Hey, Kendall," he says. "I was just...."

"Getting me flowers," I say, finishing his thought that I can clearly read.

"Yeah, well, you know. I thought it would be a nice gesture and all."

I walk about to his left and lightly pass my hand over a bundle of fresh lavender. It's almost a sweet, smoky smell, yet at the same time, it reminds me of a birthday cake my Grandma Ethel made for me when I was nine years old when she steeped dried lavender into a tea and used it in the icing.

"The stuff grows crazy in the south of France," I say, not knowing where the information suddenly came from. That's my brain, though. Flashes of knowledge spring up at me with little or no warning.

"In Marseilles," Jason says, shrugging. "I heard Taylor talking about it. It's supposed to help you sleep or something like that."

I haven't actually had a good night's rest since the whole Dojo Disturbance started. Maybe a sprig or two of this stuff would do me some good.

I reach to pluck a bundle and my fingers bump into Jason's, going for the same bunch. I try to pull back, but he snags my hand in his. His beautiful blue eyes darken slightly as he begs me with them, urging me to take him back.

"I can't, Jason," I say, barely above a whisper.

A passing bicyclists whizzes to close to us and I jump a bit. Jason instinctively wraps his arm around me. I enjoy the protection, though only momentarily. I've moved past needing him to be my savior, guardian, and knight in shining armor. Nowadays, I save myself.

"Kendall…."

I shake my head and step away from his touch. "I'll always care about you, Jason. Always. You'll be my first love, like, for the rest of my life. No one can take that away from us. But things happened. You left. I changed. You withdrew. I found someone else. I never meant to hurt you or lead you to believe we still had a chance." I take in a deep, deep breath for courage. "I'm in love with Patrick. Like, totally and completely."

"I know," he says.

"You're a great guy, Jason. You won't have trouble finding someone else."

He snickers at me. "You're a tough act to follow."

I scrunch up my face. "Isn't that a line from *Superman 2?*"

Jason tosses his head back and laughs. "I can't get anything past you."

"I don't know why you'd try."

He gathers me to him again for a bear hug. This time, there's nothing romantic or wanting about it at all. Instead, it's an embrace between friends. Two people who'll always be there for each other.

Jason digs into his pocket and pulls out a few euro coins. He goes over and pays the shop lady and then takes a small bunch of the lavender and hands it over to me.

"You didn't have to…."

"I wanted to," he says. "You need your sleep, Kendall. We've got a hell of a fight ahead of us with this piece of work, Christian Campbell. We're going to need you in tip top shape."

I take the flowers and press them to my nose. "Thanks, Jase."

He's right. The battle has yet to begin.

CHAPTER SIXTEEN

Remarkably, I have one of the best nights of sleep that I've had in a long time. Aunt Andi and I steeped some of the fragrant lavender in a tea for me that I drank with a little sugar. Then, I placed some of the stems under my pillow and did some deep breathing to try and relax and try to wipe my obsessive thoughts of Christian Campbell out of my mind. Next thing I knew, the alarm was going off and the sun was peeking through the sheer curtains of our room.

I stretch my arms over my head and wiggle my feet underneath the covers. Slowly, I withdraw from the sheets and pad over to the window. I swing open the shutters and take in the dewy freshness of the early morning. A French flag flaps in the breeze just above my balcony, reminding me of where I am—so far away from home. Pigeons flap around on the adjacent roof tops and the market street below begins to come alive with merchants opening up for another day of business.

And today, I'm not a psychic kid or part of Christian Campbell's entourage. Today, I'm just... *moi*.

"How are you feeling?" Aunt Andi asks from underneath the mound of pillows on her bed.

"I'm... great," I say with confidence. "Nothing like a fourteen-hour low grade coma."

She laughs. "You missed out on a fun evening, but rest was the most important thing for you."

I plop down on the end of her bed and tuck my feet up underneath me. "What did you guys do?"

"We took a bateaux down the Seine."

"A bateaux? What's that?"

"One of those long, glass boats that float down the river," my aunt explains. "We started at the Eiffel Tower and cruised all the way down to Notre Dame. It was breathtaking."

I bite my lip at bit at missing out on the touristy stuff.

"Taylor couldn't stop taking pictures of everything we saw along the way. That girl has an amazing eye," Andi says. "Some of her shots last night were gorgeous. I could do a whole display in my gallery based on her talent."

"That would be cool."

Andi pulls herself up out of bed. "In fact, I have a meeting with a gallery today to try and get one of their exhibits over to St. Louis. Everyone was talking about doing the tourist thing today if you're up to it."

Exhilaration races through my body. "Oh, hell yeah!" I'm in Paris and I want to see *everything*. No regrets. No looking back in ten years wishing I'd done this, that, or the other thing.

I shower, dress, and head downstairs to the restaurant where my friends are. Taylor is sipping a café and studying a Paris Metro map. Celia and Jason have their heads bent together talking about a new piece of ghost hunting equipment she ordered from DigitalDowsing.com. I don't want to talk shop right now. I want to be immersed in everything that Paris has to offer.

A warm hand slides across my waist and I jump a bit at the contact.

"Hey, babe," Patrick says to me softly. Ahh, good. He's not still mad at me. "I missed you last night."

"Sorry," I say. "I had to have a major system shut down. I'm good now, though."

His smile is heartwarming as it spreads across his face. "Taylor and I planned out the whole day. All you need is a Metro pass."

I return his excitement with a grin of my own. "Then what are we waiting for?"

⚜ ⚜ ⚜

I've ridden the L in Chicago, the Tube in London, and MARTA in Atlanta, but they're not anything like the Paris Metro. Each station is unique and a work of art in and of itself. Street performers entertain in the tunnels and entrances, playing beautiful music to entertain passersby. I sense a lot of transient souls surrounding us in the underground; however, I shut my eyes to them. Now's not the time to try and help the spirits of Paris. I'm just an American teenager with her friends, enjoying all that the city has to offer.

We leave our Metro station, Ecole Militaire, and enjoy pretty much every highlight of Paris. We spend several hours in the Louvre—I could stay there a year alone—marveling at the massive portraits, statues, and centuries old artwork. I'll admit the wait in line to see the Mona Lisa was a bit disappointing. She's not as big as I'd hoped. The Venus de Milo... wow! That's a different story. I gave into the eyes of the statue, nearly feeling the life of the artist as he carved her out. In my mind's eye, I see a time when she actually had arms: her right one across her torso and her left one holding up the modest cloth in front of her.

As we exit the famed museum, Patrick takes my hand and leads me on a leisurely walk through the Jardin de Tulieres. There, the flowers bloom in sweet array around us, providing a bouquet of color for our jaunt. A mime dressed as Charlie Chaplin stands nearby entertaining visitors. I laugh when Celia and Jason join him by mimicking the famous silent star's Little Tramp walk. Those two! Nice to see Jason enjoying himself and not being so pensive.

The rest of our morning consists of a climb to the top of the Arc de Triumph. I totally block out the residual memories of Hitler and the German army standing under the arc, proclaiming victory in Paris. Squeezing my eyes shut, I don't actually believe I see the tiny dictator. Rather, it's just recorded memories of the event that are engrained in the fabric of the city. During this, I can't help but feel like I'm being watched... monitored, almost. I flip my head around, looking for Anona. Then again, she told me she couldn't come this far with me. Who knew ghosts had barriers?

My mind wanders to Princess Di. Has she followed me over the English Channel? I can't sense her near like I did when I was in London. What I can pick up, though, is that Oliver, Christian, and Jayne are across the river at a private gallery reading. Clearly, I can visualize Christian and his Ouija board sitting in front of a crowd of wide-eyed French people who've paid to see if the psychic can connect with their lost relatives. There's Jayne, still glued to Christian's side. And Oliver's beaming pride in the front row as the audience claps along with Christian's revelations.

A tender hand on my shoulder knocks me back to where I am with my group. Celia's eyes gentle toward mine. "You okay, Kendall? I asked if you wanted to go over to Notre Dame and you didn't answer."

"Sorry, I was having a vision."

She winces. "Hmm, I don't need to have your powers to know that Christian's still up to his same old crap. Only a new audiences."

"Hell is empty and all the devils are here," I state.

Celia's mouth falls open and she cracks up. "Oh, not you did'unt! Girlfriend just threw down *The Tempest* gauntlet! Touché, my friend, touché."

I love tweaking Celia with Shakespeare and it works to lighten the mood.

"So, whattaya say we go view Paris from a higher vantage point," she says.

Minus a few euros later and a long wait in line, we make the climb to the top of Notre Dame for an up-close and personal visit with the ancient gargoyles that hang from the building, as well as the bell tower made famous in *The Hunchback of Notre Dame*. After that, we head over to the village of Montmartre and check out La Basilique du Sacre Coeur. I giggle at myself walking through these streets, imagining that I'm Satine from the *Moulin Rouge* walking along with Patrick, the guy I love, hand in hand—only without the whole dying of consumption and bursting into song thing.

Another Metro ride finds us at the Pompidou Centre in the fourth arrondisssment. Look at me, getting good with my Paris directions.

"What is *this* place?" Celia asks, wide-eyed.

Jason's mouth drops open. "I've never seen anything so cool."

Taylor reads from her tour book. "The Centre Georges Pompidou houses *Bibliothèque publique d'information* and the *Musee National d'Art Moderne.*"

Celia snorts. "A library and museum of modern art."

Pointing at the structure, Jason remarks. "But check out the architecture."

I can read Celia's mind as her eyes dance over the original building, taking in all of the details. The intricate weave of pipes and fixtures of the outside of the building make it appear as though the place has been turned inside out. Plumbing pipes, climate control ducts, electrical casings, air circulation elements, and safety devices have all been weaved together in a most modern artsy way.

"Let's go check it out," she says to Jason, and the two of them geek off together in architecture appreciation land.

Patrick decides to go inside for a bit and I choose to I walk around with Taylor as she snaps pictures of the modern building. Close-ups of the pipes, abstracts of the wiring, and crazy angles of the sun hitting the glass panels.

"Aunt Andi's really impressed with your photograph," I tell her. I touch her arm and I'm suddenly propelled into Taylor Tillson's future. She's surrounded by cameras, lights, assistants, and investors wanting to support her art. "You're going to be famous."

She giggles at me and tosses her hair back. "I just love taking pictures. It's merely a talent... like your psychic abilities."

I dodge three little kids running toward me and then wince a bit. "I'm still coming to terms with this so-called talent."

"But you're helping others, Kendall."

"I'm trying." I think of the two failed investigations in England when Christian took over. "It's hard to help people when they're more impressed with the shine and pomp of a celebrity psychic."

Taylor flattens her mouth. "Christian."

"Yeah."

"Well, he'll get his," she says. "Mark my word."

My heartbeat triples in a cocktail of anxiety and fear. "I just don't want anyone to get hurt in the process."

Taylor turns her camera behind the center to where the sun sparkles off a large fountain of water. We walk over and check it out.

"*La Fontain Stravinsky*," she reads from the sign. It's a totally whimsical public fountain sporting sixteen extremely colorful sculptures that move and quirt water at visitors. There's a set of red lips, a frog, an elephant, a clown's hat, a mermaid, a…

Through the streams of water shooting out of the tallest of the structures, I see a couple with their heads bent together laughing and smile. They're sketching what they see and sharing their art with each other. It's…Celia and Jason.

"I didn't know Jason could draw," I note.

Taylor pulls her Nikon away from her face. "Oh, yeah, he took an art class when we were in Alaska. He's been thinking about becoming an architect. I think it's one of the reasons he wanted to come on this trip, you know, to get a look at classic structures and stuff."

In all of my own personal angst and assumptions that Jason was merely here for me, I'd totally missed that he might have his own motivations for coming along on this trip. Now who's the narcissist? And it's great that he and Celia can appreciate things together. She's always such a geek about the details and construction of things.

Patrick appears at my side. "That was wicked," he tells me. "Amazing what this city offers."

"Where to next?" I ask.

Taylor's eyes get big. "Oooo, I'd love to snap pics at Pere Lachaise Cemetery!"

"Awesome... maybe we'll run into the ghost of Jim Morrison."

❧ ❧ ❧

Okay, so no dancing Morrison apparition at the cemetery, but an incredible day all around.

That is until we get to the Rodin House and Museum.

Once I step into the perfectly manicured garden of the famed artist, I begin to get that overall sense of ickiness coating me. Not that I think Rodin was evil or that his spirit is trapped here, rather, something is reaching out to me. Trying to speak to me. Get my attention. In fact, it's been with me all day long, I realize, only I've been so distracted by my friends and the fun that I haven't let this presence pull me down.

And now it's here. Surrounding me. Wrapping arms of distraction around my brain and squeezing tightly. Screaming out for me to focus on it instead of the magnificent garden and museum I'm visiting.

Taylor's photographing the Gates of Hell display, while Jason and Celia wander off to the back of the garden to get an etching of Rodin's signature on one of the statues. I follow Patrick around to the side of the house where I suddenly find myself standing in front of The Thinker. You know, the statue of the guy seated with his head in his hands, looking almost as if he's on the toilet. I'd always found the idea of the sculpture to be quite funny until I'm in its presence. It's completely awe-inspiring due to its massive size and the fact that it's made of bronze and someone actually molded it to look like that.

The statue was created in 1880, according to the plaque, and it depicts a man totally consumed by his thoughts. He seems so much like a lost soul, someone who's unsure of where he's going or where he's been.

As I stare into the expressionless face, my familiar psychic headache begins to tap at my temples, warning me to the manifestation of a ghostly entity. The air around me shifts, the temperature cooling off near my knees and feet. The statue seems to be calling to me. Unspoken words of a person I never knew, yet someone who is very much a part of me. A voice I don't recognize, yet it sounds so familiar.

I gaze deeper and deeper into the face of the man. The tight jaw. The stern mouth. The brows set in deep concentration.

Then the façade begins to morph and change. The statue comes alive with real skin, hair, eyes that match my own. And I'm staring at someone who looks very much like...*me*.

CHAPTER SEVENTEEN

One minute I'm in the Rodin garden and the next...
   ...smoke...

...mist...

...fog...

This smoky, misty fog encompasses me and stretches out in a churning motion. When it clears, I'm transported to another place. Another time?

I'm in another country, at least.

Italy, perhaps.

A small picturesque town of cobbled alleys, porticos, and steeped streets leading up from the lake. Beautiful buildings line the lakeside in shades of every pastel color imaginable, topped with red roofs.

I'm standing on a balcony of one of these houses, overlooking an amazing, scenic sunset over a pristine, glassy lake that stretches out to the horizon. The body of water is so still, so clear, so big. It almost seems ocean-like, but I know it's not.

Mountaintops paint triangular peaks in the distance. A flock of birds dip low over the water in their race toward... somewhere.

The aroma of rich, freshly brewed coffee wafts from the charming Italian villa behind me.

Silence is broken by the passing buzz of a motor boat slicing through the tranquil water and tossing it v-like aside, as it leaves foamy white caps in its wake. An older couple riding on the boat wave out and I lift my hand in return.

Turning, I walk—or maybe I float—across the deck into a beautifully appointed bedroom with a handmade antique quilt of patchwork fabric draped around the canopy post. I don't know whose room this is, yet it feels homey and familiar to me.

Have I slept here?

I make my way deeper into the villa, spacious with plenty of chaises, chairs, artwork, vases, and terra cotta pots filled with greenery stretching up to the ceiling.

Glancing around, I recognize that I've had this vision before. This is a vision, right?

I'm definitely in Italy.

And I know my maternal grandparents—Emily Faulkner's parents—are near.

Was that them on the boat?

How can I be in Italy, though? I was just in Paris.

If I'm having some sort of out of body experience or astral projection, then I don't need to waste time. I need clues. Information. A street name. An address.

I plunder through a stack of mail sitting on a nearby cabinet. Damn, I wish I knew Italian!

Outside the kitchen window, there's a road marker. Squinting hard, I try to make out the words printed on the sign. I must remember this: *Strada Provinciale 42.* I can't forget!

Then, fingers of guidance beckon me deeper into the house, back to a sun-filled room with large sunflowers blooming tall next to the open window. Before I know it, I'm enveloped in the warm embrace and bosom of an older woman rocking me back and forth.

"It's going to be okay, dear," she tells me.

I open my mouth to speak, but nothing comes out.

Emotions threaten to strangle me until I feel myself passing out.

Blackness.

Stillness.

Quiet.

I awaken, lying on a bench back at the Rodin garden. Patrick's strong hands grip me by the shoulder as he shakes me slightly.

"Kendall? Can you hear me?"

"Shouldn't we call 911?" Celia asks.

"I don't think they call it that here," Taylor notes. "I think it's 112."

"Whatever," Jason snaps. "We need to get her to a doctor."

Patrick's voice, smooth and calm through the panic, reaches out to me. "No, this isn't medical. She'll be okay in a minute." Then he gazes down at me and my eyes sync with his dark brown ones. "Right, babe? You're coming out of this, aren't you?"

With another small shake from Patrick, I seem to snap out of it. The mist and haze is gone; taking with it the breathtaking lake country and the kind woman who held me in her arms. Patrick's grip tightens to return me to this reality. He's not mad at me or anything, but I know he's trying to anchor me back in my own skin.

"Where'd you go?" he asks softly.

I swallow hard at the lump in my throat. "Italy. A lake. A villa. An address." I sit up, holding on to Patrick as he assists. Celia sits next to me immediately and hands me a bottle of water. "Thanks, Cel."

The memories of the vision—or projection, or whatever—collide in my brain like they're being crushed in an atom smasher. Everything rearranges and forms incorrectly. Colors, shapes, and furniture. The address. What address? My temple pounds and my heart races like the bounding waves kicked up by my fictitious motor boat. Why can't I remember it?

Tears stain my vision and frustration speeds through my blood stream. My breathing hitches as I begin to weep relentlessly.

Patrick gathers me to him and shushes me. "It's going to be okay, Kendall."

I sip in air. "No... no... no... not if I can't remember. Wh-wh-what's the point of all of this if I can't *remember?*"

I was there. I was close. Emily's parents. My grandparents.

They were right there.

"Drink something, Kendall," Celia tells me and I obey.

Jason has brought me a damp paper towel and Taylor uses it to wipe the back of my neck.

I try hard to make my breathing calm the hell down, but all I can see is a tornado cloud of confusion and frustration over trying to get that address back.

I can't recall that stupid Italian street name to save my life.

Why? Why!

Patrick cups my chin with his hand and smiles at me. "*Strada Provinciale 42.*"

I start to laugh, then cry more, then laugh again before I dive onto him with an all-out hug.

My connection with him binds us together even when I'm in some sort of dream trance.

He firmly says, "We'll find them, I promise."

And somehow, I know we will.

⚜ ⚜ ⚜

"Ahhhhhh! I can't believe you're finally here!" I hear screamed out at me after we emerge from the République Mètro station and make our way into the crowd gathered for the festivities.

Becca Asiaf dives down from the small stage where her DJ equipment is set up and nearly crowd surfs down onto me, Celia, and Taylor. The three of us hug like long-lost sisters and it's so good for our ghost huntress team to be back together.

"Where have y'all been?" Becca asks. "I've been texting you for two days."

Taylor looks at her iPhone. "What? I haven't gotten anything."

"It's paranormal," I say, jokingly.

Celia fingers her hair behind her ears. "We've been doing the tourist thing."

Becca, not as Gothed out as usual, is wearing a silver sparkly tank top, about forty bracelets, long, dangly earrings, and a pair of cutoff jeans. Her hair is pulled up in a high ponytail and she's positively glowing.

"You wear Paris well," I say.

"I know! I effing love it here. I never want to go back to Radisson."

Taylor gasps. "But you're going to, right?"

Becca rolls her eyes. "Umm...duh." Then she turns her attention to Celia. "G'friend, you look awesome. Love the eye shadow and haircut. You must be in love 'cause you radiate."

Celia blushes ten shades of red and then waves Becca off. "I so do not."

"Yeah... you do."

"Give me a break. I just got a lot of sun these past few days."

"Whatever." Becca knocks me with her elbow. "You're the psychic, Kendall. What do you think?"

I dance my eyes over my friend and do notice how pretty she looks in her off the shoulder draped black blouse and jean mini skirt that shows off her long legs. When she said something to me about all the guys on the trip being after me, I hope she wasn't hinting that she was interested in Christian. Celia's got better smarts than that. I hope. "Hey, she's a free agent, so whatever makes her happy," I say.

Becca gathers us around again. "Well, all y'all make me happy. I'm super psyched that you're here. This is my third night spinning for the DanceFest part of the *Paris La Fête de la Musique.*"

"*Très bien,*" Taylor says. "I see the French is wearing off on you."

"*Oui,*" Becca says with a laugh. She glances past us and sees the guys. "Hey, Jase, great to see you. And, hey, Patrick."

Both guys wave at her. They seem more interested in the street fair going on around us, filled with performance artists, music, vendors selling every kind of food imaginable, and the free performances on everything from jazz to hip-hop, electronica, House, and Dance.

"Are y'all hungry?" Becca asks. "There are gyros stuffed with frites over there, falafels from the Jewish neighborhood food carts, crepes galore, and any kind of pastry you could want. The chocolate éclairs over there will curl your hair."

We all laugh and I tell Becca, "We ate at this awesome bistro near our hotel called Café du Marche" Mmm... roasted chicken, potatoes, salad, and fresh bread…doesn't sound so spectacular, but it was ambrosia for only a few euros.

"You won't go hungry here," she tells us.

A tall guy with jet black hair, at least three days of stubble, and clear green eyes interrupts with a hand on my friend's shoulder. "Rebecca, it is time to get back to work."

"Oh, right. This is Alain, y'all. He's from Nice. Which is nice, huh?" Her nervous laughter lets on to me that he's a lot more than a mere acquaintance. I see them together in the south of France frolicking in the Mediterranean Sea and kissing on the beach. Glad to see she hasn't been pining away for Brett, aka Dragon, back home while she's been in the City of Love all summer. Perhaps there's something in the air here that makes people just want to… celebrate life.

"Pleased to meet you all," Alain says with a thick French accent. "*Oui,* we must start, Rebecca."

She waves at us and then disappears back up onto a small stage area where the electronic music is blaring from. Patrick wraps his arm around my waist and we blend into the crowd to watch the DJs perform. There stands Becca in all her glory; in her true element. She's got the headphones wrapped around her neck and is spinning a mix of dub step with a classic Beatles tune. She looks like a model straight from the Paris runways. Glamor, glitz, and googliness over Alain, who's standing nearby, cheering her on.

Wow, she is vibrantly happy. It's written all over her face.

I lean back into Patrick's strong chest and close my eyes as the music flows around me. The rhythm reaches out to my very soul, making me tap my sandaled feet. The smooth beat Becca spins blends into a mellow groove with the grinding club drum bass. I laugh in spite of myself. Who knew I knew so much about Dance music? Becca's taught me a lot.

"The crowd is digging her mix," Patrick says near my ear.

"She's amazing."

As her concert progresses, the crowd begins to dance unabashed, and we join in with the melee of waving hands and arms.

Patrick actually moves to the groove with me, spinning me around in front of him as he holds our joined hands high. Becca waves out to us and we take tons of pics of her as we cheer her on. Taylor's snapping away and I even get some video on my camera phone. I can't wait to post these all over Facebook and Twitter. Dragon's going to kick himself for letting beautiful Becca go so easily.

After a few pumping songs, Becca slows things down with a chill out tempo to get everyone close. The street lights adjust to a lower hue and you can literally feel that romance is in the air. Patrick pulls me to him and we dance together. I weave my fingers around his neck and up into his thick hair. He nuzzles my shoulder with his chin, softly humming along to the music. I breathe in the scent of him, spicy from his cologne, yet warm and boy-sweaty from the summer heat. I love being in his arms, feeling protected and loved. Even though he hasn't actually said the three meaningful, magical words, he's still the best boyfriend.

I turn to look over at Taylor who's found some hot French friend of Alain's to dance with and… I do a double-take. Are Celia and Jason slow dancing? Together?

I cock my head a bit and peer over Patrick's shoulder to see my gangly, gorgeous, geeky friend absolutely beaming as she looks up (and it's a big deal for Celia Nichols to look up at someone) into Jason Tillson's blue eyes. The same Dasani-blue ones I once gazed into the exact same way.

She's not wearing makeup for Christian Campbell… she's doing it for Jason!

It's like I've been smacked in the face with a cold glass of iced tea. Celia once had a massive crush on Jason before I came to town and now she—*hey, they're kissing!*

"Oh, my God! Jason and Celia are totally making out," I exclaim to Patrick.

He turns. "So they are."

Umm, yes they are! Right here in Paris. The city of love.

Right here in front of me!

Wait a second…

For a moment, my heart cracks and aches as I watch my former boyfriend and my best friend together, apparently quite into each other from the way things are progressing. Suddenly, Patrick tightens his grip on me as if to remind me of where I am and who I'm with.

Oh, right. This is a good thing.

What two better people than Celia and Jason? They've known each other since they were little kids, have grown up together, and share so many common interests. Some psychic I am, since I never saw this one coming.

A crazy big smile crosses my face and I breathe a sigh of relief. My heart stitches back together quickly and the moisture on the rim of my eyes isn't for any kind of loss or jealousy, rather it's from a joy that Celia and Jason have found each other.

I nudge Patrick. "I had absolutely no idea."

He tilts his head down and kisses me deeply, touching my soul with his. When he pulls back he says, "Yeah, well... I did."

CHAPTER EIGHTEEN

The next day, our group meets up with Becca, Alain, his friend, Rémy—who Taylor swooned over all night—at the park next to the Eiffel Tower, *Parc du Champ de Mars*. Look at me getting all French and stuff. When we arrive after the short walk from Rue Cler, we see Becca's toting a huge picnic basket and Rémy's carrying three French baguettes like they're military rifles on his shoulder.

"I hope y'all are hungry," Becca shouts out to us.

"I'm famished," Taylor responds.

Celia steps back from me. She's been a little standoffish since last night's DanceFest. Even though I smiled brightly at Jason and her together, I can see that my friend is feeling a little bit of guilt at hooking up with my ex. It really doesn't matter. I'm happy for them. Really, I am.

"We okay?" I ask her as we help Becca spread out the large blanket over the lush green grass. "Wasn't last night great?"

She glances over at me and a slight pink blush crosses her cheeks. "It was. Kendall, I need to tell you—"

"You and Jason hooked up. I know. I saw. I'm thrilled."

Her eyes grow huge. "You are?"

"Of course. As you said, I can't have all the guys on this trip."

She shakes her head. "Kendall, I never meant—"

I take her hands in my and bounce them up and down. "It's totally cool. You guys look awesome together. I just want you to be happy."

Celia launches at me and hugs me like she's never hugged me before.

"Now what?" Jason asks.

I sneer at him. "You think something's wrong just 'cause we hug."

He nods. "When girls hug, it means something's happened."

Okay, Jason. "Yep. You guys happened. And I'm very happy for you."

Now Jason blushes as he shifts his eyes over to Celia. She reaches out her hand and meets his halfway in the air space between them. I grin broadly at them.

"I love it. Come on, let's eat!"

Taylor dances in place. "And then let's climb to the top of the Eiffel Tower."

"And spit off the top," Becca says cheekily.

"I can't wait to see what the world looks like from up there," I say dreamily.

Patrick lowers himself down to the blanket and pats at the spot next to him. I plop down and reach forward to grab a grape off the platter Becca's setting out. There are several cheeses, deli meats, sliced apples, grapes, carrots, bread, and a huge box of pastries. She also breaks out a couple of... wine?"

"Umm, Becca, aren't we a little young to be drinking?" I ask.

"Technically, Alain is old enough to drink because he's eighteen. However, this is not alcoholic. This is club soda with grenadine flavored Sirop Teisseire in it. It's a totally French drink and I thought it would do in place of champagne."

"What are we celebrating?" Taylor asks as she sits down next to Rémy.

"Life," Becca says, raising her plastic cup high. "To good friends, a beautiful summer day, the opportunity to be here, and to all the lost souls we've been commissioned to help."

I swallow hard as the fizzy-syrupy drink suddenly sours in my mouth. I feel my pulse pick up as disappointment in my own cowardice cascades over me. As lovely as this picnic is—we're sitting under the Eiffel Tower...hello!—we shouldn't be here. We shouldn't have wasted the last two days being tourists when Christian Campbell is still out there somewhere spewing his garbage on an unwitting public who easily parts with their money for the wannabe TV talent to tell them things they already know.

I set my cup down. "We have to go back."

Patrick turns to look at me. "I've been thinking the same thing."

"Back where?" Becca asks as she breaks off a piece of the baguette.

"To the tour with Oliver... and Christian Campbell."

Alain's brow lifts. "The Scottish teen psychic? He was on Métropole 6, one of our TV stations, yesterday afternoon. My *grand-mère* is going to his psychic reading at the Ritz."

"Are you kidding me?" I shout.

"What's the deal with this kid?" Becca asks.

We catch her up on everything that transpired in London and since we got to Paris.

I pick at a piece of brie on my plate. "It was wrong to leave and let Christian get his way. Oliver's judgment is clouded about Christian and I should have tried harder. I shouldn't have left Jayne. I should have protected her more."

Becca flattens her lips. "Then do something about it. You're frickin' Kendall Moorehead. You've taken on a hell of a lot more than some fame-hungry, self-aggrandizing Scot. You've dealt with malevolent spirits who've hurt your dad, pushed you down a staircase, damn near killed you, and did kill our friend, Farah. This Christian kid is a piece of cake."

Turning to Patrick, I snicker. "She makes it sound so easy."

Jason draws himself up from his stretched out position and pops the last bite of his cheese and bread into his mouth. He withdraws his tablet computer from his backpack and fires it up. "Actually, Kendall, it might just be that easy."

Now I lift a brow. "What are you talking about?"

Celia stops chewing. "Jason and I stayed up late last night doing some research on our little friend Christian."

I slant my eyes toward her. Yeah, research... between make out sessions.

"What did you find?" Patrick asks, intrigued.

Jason taps on his screen a bit and then turns the tablet around. "I was thinking about this alleged 'Dojo Disturbance,' so I Googled around some. Turns out this disturbance is for real. Or at least there's a bit of a world-wide epidemic of reports of a spirit using this name."

Nabbing the tablet, Celia clicks on a bookmark they saved. "It seems that these reports stem from a particular type of tree that's on the border of Germany and France. A company made Ouija boards from these trees and sold them throughout Europe to kids in the 1960s and 1970s as toys."

Becca tosses her head back. "Who wants to play dress-up with Barbie when you can communicate with Satan?"

"Seriously," I say, sarcastically. "So what about these boards from this tree?"

Jason reads on. "The trademark is owned by Hasbro back in the states, but other companies make similar boards in the same manner to be used as a 'parlor game.'"

"I think I prefer gin rummy," Taylor says quietly.

Celia reads: "One of the first mentions of using a Ouija board is found in 1100 AD China historical documents of the Song Dynasty. The method was known as *fuji* or 'planchette writing.' It means ostensibly contacting the dead and the spirit-world, and, albeit under special rituals and supervisions, was a central practice until it was forbidden by the Qing Dynasty."

She's starting to make my head hurt. "What does this have to do with Christian?"

"We're getting to that," Jason says. "See, the word 'Ouija' comes from the combined French and German words for 'yes' – *oui* and *ja*. A lot of the original boards were actually made in both countries until Parker Brothers bought the idea. Now, Celia managed to get one of Christian's prized boards before we left his company."

"Celia! You stole it?" Taylor exclaims.

"Sort of."

Becca leans over and fist bumps Celia. I merely smile.

"I looked at the board and saw a name on the board," Celia says. "It said Nuremberg, Germany. So, I did a little more digging. Seems that tilia trees are prominent in this area of Germany. Manufacturers use tilia sawdust to make medium-density fiber board."

I squeeze my eyes shut. "You're making my head hurt. What does this have to do with Christian?"

"Be patient, Kendall," Jason says, standing up for Celia. She smiles at him.

"Sorry... go ahead."

"Ouija boards are made from MDF, or medium-density fiber board. Most are now produced for cheap in China—"

"—just like everything else," Patrick quips.

"—but these older boards, the ones people are claiming the Dojo Disturbance on, come from those original tilia trees in Germany," Celia says. "It gets better though."

Jason lights up. "Oh, this is the best part!"

Blinking hard, I listen up.

Celia taps the tablet again and pulls up a genealogy website. "I hacked a little more and found that back in the 1950s, a particular tilia farm in Nuremburg was owned by a man named Henrik Anderson who willed it to his adopted son from his Scottish war bride, Anderson MacLeod from East Kilbride, Scotland."

Jason takes over. "Seems that this MacLeod was a magician back in the 1970s who stirred up trouble throughout the UK at county fairs. Had quite a rep as a fraud and con artist, trying to get money from people by predicting their futures with his Ouija board."

This is all very interesting, but I'm not sure where they're going. I'm totally impressed that they spent so much time, but as to how this relates to Christian...wait a second...my psychic headache taps at my left temple and my eye begins to twitch.

"Christian is from East Kilbride," I say, as if knowing it for a fact.

Celia points an apple slice at me. "Bingo. Give that woman more sparkling soda."

I rub my head with my hand to massage away the pain. "Okay, so what if he's from the same town?"

A snicker escapes from Jason's lips. "Our research shows that Christian Campbell is merely a stage name. Seems that our salon-highlighted-hair friend is really Andrew Christian MacLeod, grandson of Anderson MacLeod."

Patrick claps his hands together. "Snap!"

My mouth drops open. "I was right! He's a fraud! A scam!"

"Just 'cause he's using a pseudonym doesn't make him a fake," Celia points out. She has a point, yet still, something doesn't add up.

Taylor nods her head. "We've got to do something."

"Damn right we do," I say. "We have to get this information to Oliver Bates immediately or not only will he lose his TV show and his reputation, but someone's bound to get hurt!"

Our climb to the top of the Eiffel Tower will have to wait.

⚜   ⚜   ⚜

Forty-five minutes later, we arrive at the Hotel Ritz in Place Vendrôme in the first arrondissment on the right bank. The second we walk up the red carpeted steps and spin into the lobby through the revolving door, splattered images appear to me like a slide show on speed. I see socialites and diplomats, rich tourists and French businessmen. All people who've passed through these doors. In the lobby, I glance up at the glittering, gorgeous chandelier that dangles overhead. Across the marbled floor, a rich red-carpeted staircase leads up, dividing to go up to the left and the right.

Standing at the top left, gripping the black railing is... Princess Diana.

I gasp at seeing her again, my hands flying to my throat in disbelief. At least, it looks like her. Maybe it's just another spirit taking her form, but... no. The Hotel Ritz was the last place the princess was photographed alive. I've seen the video of her in the back elevator with the driver of her car, Henri Paul and her boyfriend/fiancé,

Dodi Fayed. Yes, I know all about it because I've read every book and seen every documentary about Diana's life. I can't believe I'm actually in the hotel where everything happened. Flashes of that night hit me like homerun balls. *Diana and Dodi in the back elevator. Getting into the black Mercedes Benz. Driving too fast. Outrunning the paparazzi. Too, too fast. A bad dip in the road. The car flips. It smashes into the pilon. Screams. Blood. Pain. Heartache.*

"Are you okay, Kendall?" Patrick asks with concern in his voice.

"She's here again. Can you see her?"

"Princess Di?"

I nod. Patrick shakes his head.

My fingers jam into my hair and I rub hard at the images. Ones I'd seen on the news reports and online, but now they seem so real, as if they just happened all over again. I glance up at where the Princess stands on the stairs gazing down at me with her caring blue eyes. I so admire everything she stood for... all the charity work, caring for the poor, and perhaps here to help me?

Is this the spirit protector Anona was referring to?

Maybe this really *is* the Princess of Wales.

She lifts her stern chin and gestures with her head for me to move deeper into the hotel. I read her thoughts. She wants me to go into one of the grand salons where Christian is conducting his gallery reading. Ironically, it's in a room called "Psyché."

"This way," I say to everyone.

I try not to think of all the famous people who've crossed these hallways...not wanting to connect with their residual energy right now. Diana is the only spirit I need to see. She's showing me the way.

We slip into the room, trying not to cause a ruckus. There, we find Christian is in full performance mode with the TV cameras rolling. That didn't take much effort on Oliver's party.

Christian points at an elderly woman in the front row who is in a wheelchair. Just as he did in London, he leans down to her and tells her, "I'm sensing some health issues."

Celia snorts and says, "Really? Is that the shtick he's sticking with?"

"It worked before," Jason mutters.

Princess Diana materializes close to me, so much so that I can smell her powdery perfume. She lifts her delicate hand and points in the direction of where I see Jayne Mcburney sitting in the audience. She pushes her glassed up her nose as she's taking notes and gazing adoringly at Christian.

"You have to save her," the princess says to me. "You must."

I look at the innocent girl, so full of admiration for this fake. The spirit of Diana is right. Jayne has to be protected at all costs.

This summer hasn't exactly gone as planned, so I wonder, is this why I'm on this journey?

Princess Diana nods at me and fades away.

My psychic senses tell me that everything is about to be revealed.

CHAPTER NINETEEN

I watch as Christian prances across the stage. And yes, it's a prance. A preen. A posturing. Positioning and probably a hundred other "p" words that boil down to rhyming with "t" that stands for trouble. His hair and makeup—I can see he's wearing base and powder for the camera—is perfect and his black silk shirt shows off his tanned neck. On the back of his shirt, he has silver embroidered angel wings. As if! All part of the good act, though.

He opens his eyes and folds his fingers together as he points at a woman in the audience. She stands and hands him something. I can't see at first, but then I notice it's a Ouija board.

"Great… here we go," I mutter to my friends.

Patrick places his hand on my knee to calm me.

Let's see what he's up to.

No good. We should stop him now.

We have to talk to Oliver and handle this professionally.

Whatever.

Patrick squeezes my knee and I just scowl as Christian asks his "assistant Jayne" to join him on the stage.

I fiercely want to protect her like a momma bear protecting her cub. I can't, though. Our team agreed to see how this plays out first.

"Jayne and I will attempt to communicate with the spirits using this device," Christian announces to the room of one hundred listeners.

I see that Jayne's small fingers are trembling as she touches the planchette. Christian's hands join on the item, as well. The cameraman moves forward, kneeling in the front to, no doubt, get a good close zoom shot.

Head tipped back and eyes closed, Christian asks out, "What is your name?"

The planchette slides across the glossy MDF board—damn Celia and her information overload!—with Jayne calling out the letters.

"D. O. J. O." She gasps roughly at the last one.

Christian smiles. "Ahh… my old friend, Dojo. You are here with us tonight after all. Come forward and be heard."

"I can't take this anymore," I say firmly. Patrick tries to hold me in my seat, however, the adrenalin is flowing through me like a raging river and I break free. I charge down the middle aisle, unnoticed. That is, until I scream out, "You're a fraud!"

Every head in the place turns to me. I feel a hundred sets of eyes on me, including the shocked ones of Oliver Bates on the front row.

Christian merely sneers at me. "Is there something I can help you with, Ms. Moorehead?"

Teeth gritted, I say once again, "You. Are. A. Fraud, Christian. Or should I call you Andrew Christian MacLeod!"

The fake-and-bake tan of Christian's fades on his ashen face. He levels his stare at me and I can almost see the smoke coming from his ears over his instant anger and irritation at me. He knows I'm on to him, so let the real show begin.

"You're taking advantage of these people who are grieving the loss of loved ones. You're preying on their emotions and charging them for false hopes and information."

I move up the aisle to gasps of horror and a few tears. Still, I have to do what I have to do. "Admit it, *Andrew MacLeod*, you and your family made up this alleged Dojo Disturbance just so you can get an international tour and your own television show."

Christian's mouth literally drops open. Jayne's does too as the Ouija board falls to the stage.

Oliver stands to head me off. "Kendall, this isn't the place—"

"Yes it is! Shame on you, Oliver, for encouraging this. He's nothing but an imposter."

Christian screams out, "Security!"

Oliver rushes over to Christian and Jayne and sweeps them away back stage.

Before I know what's happening, two large men in black suits move in, take me by the arms, and drag me out of the ballroom.

"Patrick! Help me!"

❧ ❧ ❧

I'm unceremoniously shoved into the expansive suite where Oliver, Christian, and Jayne are waiting for me.

Immediately, Patrick and our friends spill into the room to defend my honor. "Kendall, you're not hurt, are you?" Patrick asks.

I rub my arm where one of the gorillas manhandled me. "I'm okay."

Oliver is anything but fine. From the bulge of the vein at his temple and his red face, I'd say he's fuming. He lifts his hand and for a split second, I actually think he's going to take a whack at me for ruining this TV show that he and Christian have been working on.

He surprises me, though, by pointing his wrath at the Scottish teen. "This is all true, isn't it?"

I slump against a nearby chair in relief.

Christian advances. "She's poisoned you against me. She's turned you all against me."

Celia snorts. "Dude, I never liked you."

"Me, either," Jason adds.

Taylor and Patrick shake their heads and Becca laughs. "I just got here and I think you're a piece of crap."

Christian is livid. He knocks over the lamp on the table next to the couch. "You've ruined everything!"

"No, Christian. You've done it to yourself and you tried to drag us all down with you," I say. "Especially Oliver, who put his trust in you."

Oliver stands aside rubbing his head. His eyes roll back into his head and I know his psychic abilities are taking over. "I didn't want to see this. I could have seen it, but I didn't."

"Tell him, Christian," I say sternly.

He runs his hands through his perfectly coifed and gelled hair. "I need the money. My family's bad off. I just picked up where my grandfather left off. He did all of the research on the Ouija boards that came from the same trees in Germany. Grandfather said if he could perpetuate the myth that all of these boards together were some sort of portal that he could pass himself off as the only person on the planet who could save people from this evil, demonic activity. He died trying and never succeeded. But he didn't have the Internet and connections and television like I have." He spins to face me. "And I could have done it, if it weren't for you!"

I feel that Christian's about to dive at me. However, Jayne's tears stop him.

"I believed in you, Christian," she says in a small voice.

Christian turns to Jayne and growls at her. "You can still believe in me. I'm the same person. I still have powers."

She circles her hands and throws him off of her with the strength of ten men. As her tears gush, she screams out at him. "You were my hero and all you did was manipulate me and everyone else. All of those people in your gallery. Those were simply lies. Those people looked to you for guidance and you betrayed them all for fame and fortune."

Rage overcomes Christian and he shouts gutturally like a banshee gone mad. "Ahhhh! Grow up! All of you!" He swings his arm again; this time knocking off a blue vase from the side table. It flies three feet and shatters when it hits the hotel room wall. Taylor, who's capturing all of this on her video phone, has to jump out of the way to avoid the shards of china.

"Christian, stop!" Oliver orders.

But the fraud isn't listening, and moves to the desk chair, picking it up over his head and smashing it to the ground. Then he goes to the flat panel TV and wrenches it off the dresser. Jason and Patrick rush forward to stop him. He wrestles them off him and shoves Jason down. Horror eats at me seeing muscular, athletic

Jason Tillson knocked on his arse by the smaller Christian. Patrick tries to capture Christian's arms, but he twists out of reach and dives over to the nearby king sized bed where his bag sits.

He rummages through the bag and dumps out six, seven, eight Ouija boards, lining them all up on the mattress.

"What are you doing, Christian?" Oliver asks.

"Stay away!"

"Christian, you've lost it," I yell.

"You're going to be sorry. All of you! I am a messenger. I can conjure up this spirit to smite you all."

"Smite?" Patrick says mockingly.

Christian tips his head back as he places his fingertips on two of the boards. "Dojo! Hear my cry! Come to me. Help me defeat my enemies. Bow to my commands, Dojo!"

I shake terribly from the fear of the situation. Yet, I bravely step forward. "Christian, there's no such thing as Dojo. Stop this right now. You need help."

He glares right at me and I swear his pupils are red, glowing with hatred for me. He speaks to me slowly and distinctly in a very deep, growling voice. "*You* are the one who is going to need help."

"Who's that talking?" Celia asks, stepping away.

Oliver breathes deeply. "Christian. Stop this right now. You don't know what you're doing."

Christian laughs hysterically, long and hard, until he begins to cough. It's as though he's choking, grappling for a good, strong breath.

Jayne hurries to his side, still crying something fierce. "Christian, Oliver's right. Please stop!"

He looks up at her with remorse and his own tears in his eyes. "I don't think I can," he manages to eke out before he falls to the floor.

Princess Diana materializes in the room, and this time I'm not awed by her past celebrity. Instead, I turn pleading eyes to her, not knowing what to do.

"Protect her, Kendall. Just as I've protected you."

Before I can do anything, Jayne screams and falls back onto the bed.

And then, right before all of us, she levitates six feet into the air.

"Holy crap! Now what do I do?"

CHAPTER TWENTY

We all stand gape-mouthed as Jayne hovers over the hotel bed. No one is more horrified than Christian. He scrambles up off the floor and cowers back in the corner. "What's going on? Jayne! Stop that! How are you doing that?"

Jayne doesn't say a word. She just growls from her gut in a low sound that can only be described as demonic.

Okay, this is *not* what I signed up for when I agreed to come on this simple summer European jaunt. I wanted history and touring, riding metros and maybe even try eating a few things I'd never had before. In no way did I plan on facing some insane teenager who'd managed to summon something sinister from the other side.

Christian claws at the wall behind him and tries to cross the room to escape.

Jason blocks his way. "You're not going anywhere, buddy."

Patrick squares up next to him, providing a muscular boy wall Christian won't penetrate. Just like him to think only about himself and to turn tail and run. We'll deal with him later. Right now, I have to worry about Jayne.

"What are you doing to her?" I ask of…whom?

Jayne's weak voice bursts through. "Help me, please."

She rises even higher off the bed, nearly six feet in the air now. A booming voice rises from her chest. "You dare trifle with me!"

Oliver takes my hand. "Who are we dealing with?"

Jayne's chest heaves and the voice bellows out. "Dojo!"

Christian swoons as he sucks in a deep breath. "It's real?"

"Yeah, bitch. Your crap is real," Becca says through gritted teeth.

"I'm not dealing with this. No way!" Christian makes a break for the door.

Quite unceremoniously, pretty Taylor trips him up and literally flips him over her shoulder, landing him on the floor with a resounding grunt.

Shock crosses Celia's face and I know it mirrors my own. "What was that?" I ask.

Taylor shrugs. "I took Tae Kwon Do when I was in Alaska."

Becca snickers. "Remind me never to tick you off."

While Christian lies there on the floor, Oliver runs into the other room. I have no idea if he's coming back or not, so I turn to Diana.

"Talk him out of her," she instructs.

"Jayne. We're here for you. You've got to fight him. Do not let him take you over." I turn to Patrick and stretch my hands out. No words need to be exchanged as we lock fingers to join our psychic abilities. Patrick is the first to address the demon.

Dojo, in the name of the Lord, I command that you leave this girl alone.

Nothing but dark laughter resonates in our heads.

My turn.

She did nothing wrong. She didn't summon you. She doesn't deserve this.

Not that I want this demon to turn his attention to Christian or anything like that. I just want this entity gone. Back to hell or purgatory or limbo or wherever.

I start praying hard, hoping God hears me and will have mercy on Jayne. It's not her fault that she wrongly trusted Christian.

Princess Diana stands nearby nodding at us. We must be doing something right.

Leave her alone, Dojo! Leave all of us alone!

Oliver dashes back into the room with a large vile of water. Holy water!

"Where did you get that?" I ask.

"I had a priest at Notre Dame bless a bunch for me. You know, in case of a rainy day."

Patrick snorts. "I think we have a hurricane on our hands."

Not wasting any more time, Oliver pops the lid off the vial and throws the holy water at Jayne's body.

She screams out as if burned, but she also drops a foot or so out of the air.

"It's working," Taylor yells out.

Oliver tosses more water at her as Patrick and I continue to hold hands, praying and demanding that Dojo leave Jayne's body. Steam sizzles off of her as the holy water does its job. She twists and fights, crying out.

"Hang in there, Jayne!"

Finally, the vial is empty of its contents and then Jayne's small body falls out of the air. Fortunately, she lands on the soft bed.

Jason and Celia run to her side immediately to see if she's okay. Jayne draws her knees up under her chin, trembling and crying at the same time.

"He's still here," Princess Di says to me. "Protect yourself, Kendall."

Patrick and I join our minds and coat ourselves in a protective bubble of white light. I feel the warmth of God taking care of me as I fight what I've been sent here to take care of.

"Where is he?" I ask to whoever can answer me.

Princess Di's eyes slice over to where the stack of Ouija boards has fallen to the floor. I break contact with Patrick and bend down to gather the offending divination tools.

"You can't take those," Christian cries.

Patrick blocks him as he moves to stop me. "Oh, hell yes, we can."

Patrick and I gather the boards and follow into the living room of Oliver's suite. Even though it's summertime, flames crackle in the fireplace. We toss the boards in and they are swiftly consumed by the hissing tongues of red, orange, and white. And then, just like that, the boards disappear in a *whoooooooooooooshing* vapor.

Patrick covers me with his body and we all duck onto the floor to avoid whatever happens next. I sense a vortex suck out the air in the room and then vanish into the fireplace like some sort of magnetic force. It takes a few seconds, but everything seems… fine.

Christian stands up and smoothes a hand over his clothes. He glares at me hatefully. "You couldn't leave well enough alone, lass, could you? You've ruined me!"

I pull up from my position on the floor and stand tall. "You ruined yourself, Christian."

Oliver's by my side and crosses his hands over his chest. "Get out of my sight. Now."

Christian returns to his room, gets his bag and slinks out, never looking back.

A collective sigh sounds out in the room.

Moving back through the suite, I gather Jayne up and hug her tightly.

"Th-th-thank you. I've never been so scared in all my life."

I stroke her hair with my hand and shush her. "It's okay."

Jayne's tear-stained eyes gaze up at me. "He wasn't the real deal. You are, Kendall."

"So are you, Jayne."

"Are you sure? I don't know if I'm really psychic," she says.

"We'll work together. I promise. You can tell me what you're going through any time."

Her eyes move about the room and then back to me. "Would you think I'm daffy if I told you that the Princess of Wales is here in the room with us?"

I crane my neck and see my friendly spirit guide still standing in the corner. She's so beautiful with her blonde hair cut stylishly around her regal face. Her blue eyes shine out and her smile is warm as she nods her approval at me.

"Yeah, she's here. She's been with me a lot on this trip."

Patrick chuckles. "I'll be damned. It is her."

Taylor, Celia, Becca, and Jason all shrug at each other.

"I don't see a thing," Becca says. "Then again, I never do."

Celia lets out a sigh. "They get to have all the fun."

I walk over and stand directly in front of the tragically deceased princess. "Are you really Diana Spencer Windsor, Princess of Wales?"

A knowing smile crosses her face and she shakes her head at me. "No, I'm not. I thought I'd approach you in a way that wouldn't frighten you."

"Why would I be frightened?" I've dealt with so many ghosts, apparitions, and lost souls, what's another one?

She laughs demurely. "I suppose I meant that I chose someone who wouldn't annoy you as much as other possibilities."

Before my eyes, the faux princess morphs into the World War II pilot that I saw at Heathrow Airport when I first landed. Then, he shifts into the dark shadow I'd seen so many times on the trip; that darkness that I thought might harm me, yet it was just a cloak for....

The spirit transforms again into a young man of maybe twenty years of age. He's wearing a denim jacket, a black T-shirt, and worn jeans. When he turns his face into mine, it's like I'm gazing into a mirror.

And it hits me.

A reality of sorts, only not.

A dream come true.

A connection with who I am.

I reach my hand to encircle my throat, hoping I can produce a sound.

"D-D-Daddy?"

Patrick gasps, as do the rest of my friends who are only hearing one side of this conversation.

The young man nods at me to let me know I have, indeed, figured things out.

"You're my father! You're Andy Caminiti!"

My birth father who died before I was born. My breathing becomes choppy and tears are close to spilling. I want to run into his arms and hug him, know the feel of his arms protecting me, but I'll meet nothing but air.

"How long have you been with me?" I ask.

"Since you found my sister," he tells me. "It was like there were some sort of spiritual bread crumbs that led me to you."

I giggle nervously at his analogy. "I wish I'd known sooner. I would have talked to you."

"I didn't have the strength or energy to appear to you at first," he says. "So, I stayed in the shadows and watched. When Anona reached out to me and said she couldn't come far with you, I thought it was best to come to you in other forms to try and help you on your journey. Until you could see the real me."

My father holds out a ghostly hand to touch my face. Even though there's no contact, I feel him. A cold tingle tickles my cheek where the tears of happiness stream down.

"I'm so proud of you, sweetie."

Patrick must sense I need him because his arms wrap around to support me.

Andy faces my boyfriend and says, "Take care of my little girl for me."

"Always," Patrick responds.

Daddy fades away. And I collapse in Patrick's arms.

Chapter Twenty-One

I step out of the hot shower, steam curling around my feet as I let it escape into the hotel room. Nothing like a cleansing myself from the paranormal ick after the encounter we had tonight.

But it was cathartic, as well.

"You okay, sweetie?" my aunt asks.

Tightening the towel around me, I lower myself to her bed and lay my wet head on her shoulder. "Yeah. I think I am."

I had told her all about seeing my father—her brother—when we first got back to the hotel. We'd cried together and laughed and hugged and cried some more.

She wraps her arms around me and softly scratches my back. "I wish I could have experienced that with you."

"Me, too."

She chuckles. "Not that I could have seen him like you did."

"You never know."

Setting me back away from her, Andi asks, "You think he's okay? In a better place?"

I shrug. "He seemed okay. But just like Emily...like my mom, once I knew who he was, he disappeared. I don't get that. If they're so concerned about me and want to be part of my life, why do they just fade away once I know who they are?"

"I don't know, sweetie."

Grabbing my brush off the nightstand, I tug it through my wet hair. "I don't know, either."

My aunt pulls off her glasses and wipes them clean on the end of her white T-shirt. As she places them back on her nose, she says, "Maybe it's just part of the journey, Kendall."

"What journey? Everyone keeps talking about my journey."

She takes the brush from me and starting working on my tangles. "Your life journey. The path you walk on that takes you to the real you. We all have a journey that makes us who we are."

"I'm only now starting to find out who I am," I tell her.

Her eyes shine as she gazes at me. "It's all part of growing up."

She knows all about my vision of Emily's parents, too. "I want to go find them."

"I figured you would."

"You think they'll freak out?"

"Only one way to find out. We'll go to Italy when you're ready. You don't have to be back in Radisson until right before school starts. Whatever we have to do, Kendall. I'm here for you."

I kiss her on the cheek, loving her so much. A few minutes later, I bite my lip a bit.

"What now?" Andi asks.

I furrow my brows. "Sometimes, I wish I were just a normal teen, you know?"

Andi tosses her head back and laughs hard. "Kendall, there's no such thing as a normal teenager. Never has been, never will be."

I suppose she's right!

❖ ❖ ❖

Since this is the last night of Becca's DJ DanceFest competition, I've gone all out. Aunt Andi curled my hair and did my makeup, giving me dark, smoky eyes and full, red lips. I put on my black fringe top and back sequin shorts to go with my rhinestone kitten heels. Long, blingy earrings finish off my look and I'm ready to go.

I join my friends in the lobby of the Grand Hotel Leveque and get a smiley pleasure at the look on Patrick's face when he sees me.

"You are one hot babe," he says, embarrassing me to the core.

Then again, he looks totally hot in his fashionable jeans black and gray skull shirt. We link hands and head off to Becca's performance.

The music is pumping and the stages are jammed when we arrive. Becca's in a short red dress with crimped hair—that totally works on her—and she's holding her headphones high as she mixes out the 808 beat.

Taylor and Rémy are dancing and Celia and Jason stand together, his arm draped over her shoulder. They look blissfully in full crush with each other and I couldn't be happier.

"Do you mind some company?" I hear next to me. I spin to see Oliver and Jayne standing there.

There's a part of me that wants to be really bitter that Oliver just ditched our summer plans all for the sake of grooming Christian. However, there's nothing to be gained by holding a grudge. Especially since Oliver was the one who brought Patrick and me together. No words need to be spoken. Oliver knows he screwed up. But hey, he's human. We all are. Mistakes happen along our journey. It's how we deal with them moving forward.

"As long as you cheer wicked loud for my friend, Becca," I say with a smile.

Oliver hugs me. "You got it." Then he says, "I want to go forward to Rome, as planned. This time, the gallery reading will be you and Patrick. You can shine."

"And Jayne," I add. "She deserves the spotlight, as well."

"Absolutely. It's a deal."

Patrick shakes his hand and then I tug Jayne over to me and make her dance with me. She giggles and stumbles a bit, but then the beat takes over and soon we're grooving together.

"Thanks for saving me, Kendall."

I wink at her. "From now on, you save yourself."

Andi slips back up with several freshly made crepes. The aroma of ham, cheese, and butter crashing together in the air makes me drool. I take one and Patrick and I share the warm treat, luxuriating in the tastes of our summer memories.

Oliver smiles at Andi and she hands a crepe to him. "Whattaya say you and I slip over to the wine bar around the corner while the kids party it up here," he asks her.

Andi raises a dark eye brow. "Like a date?"

"Sure," Oliver says. "If your niece approves."

I cock my head to the side with wonder. I thought Oliver was gay. Shows what kind of psychic I am, huh? "Go have fun. We'll be good. This goes until three a.m. and then we'll head back to the hotel."

"You sure?" Andi asks, as if I'm the adult who needs to grant permission.

Patrick says, "I'll take good care of her."

The spin off rages on and on. We dance. We sweat. We cheer. We party. We scream. And Becca wins the gold medal for her performance and a hefty prize money check. Afterwards, everyone piles on the metro over to the first arrondissment to Café Costes that's open late. It's trendy, hip, and chic, and we fit right into the scene. We have amazing French onion soup and rich, decadent chocolate cake that makes me never want to eat again because nothing could possibly top this.

"I'm fried," Taylor says. "I'm going to sleep all day tomorrow."

"Not me," Celia says. "There's a Star Wars exhibit at the Cité de Science and L'industrie that I want to go to."

"No way!" Jason pipes up. "I'm totally going with you."

She smiles brightly and they join hands again.

"My God, you two were made for each other," I tease.

Patrick moves his hand into my hair and plays with one of my long curls. "Speaking of people who were made for each other, can we slip away for a bit?"

A zizzle of excitement charges up my back. Yes. *A zizzle.*

I excuse myself from the group with the promise that Jayne will head back with them and crash in my room. The gang leaves and Patrick and I hop a cab. Where in this city, I don't know.

Before I know it, the cab lets us off in front of the Eiffel Tower. The true symbol of this entire city.

"You know, Parisians hated this structure when it was first built," I tell him.

"And now look at it."

It's completely lit up and shines before us.

"Come with me," Patrick says.

"Isn't it closed?"

A wide grin crosses Patrick's handsome face. "After what happened with Christian, Oliver owed me a favor. He knows someone who knows someone who arranged this. Come on."

Remarkably, we step over to the elevator entrance and are met by Pierre, work works there. He quietly slips us into the metal lift and zips us up to the top. My breath leaves me the second we're in the air and I can't believe what's happening.

Pierre points to the railing. "Five minutes only."

Patrick nods and leads me to the edge.

I breathe in the air and marvel at my surroundings. Words fail me other than, "This is amazing!"

My boyfriend leans down and kisses me. "You're amazing, Kendall."

"This is incredible. I can't believe we got a private visit like this. You're spoiling."

He takes my hand. "After all we've been through, I think you deserve a little spoiling me."

I reach up and stroke his cheek and then lift up on my tiptoes and kiss him. Here on the Eiffel Tower. Overlooking Paris. Whoa.

"I want to give you something."

He reaches into his pocket and pulls out a ring box. I almost gag on the intake of breath. Holy crap...we're too young to...

"It's a promise ring," he tells me and shows me the silver Irish claddagh ring—two hands clasping a heart in the middle with a crown on top. "You wear it here on your right hand with the heart facing toward your body. This means that someone has captured your heart."

"You certainly have, Patrick Lynn."

He swallows hard and I know what he's about to say. He doesn't recite it in my head, but proclaims it here to me, out loud, on top of this amazing symbol of Paris.

"I love you, Kendall. So much."

Awww!

Tears paint my eyes and I say, "I love you, too, Patrick."

And then we kiss. A perfect, end-of-the-move, romantic, sweep-me-off-my-feet, epic kiss that makes me fall deeper in love with him. His love literally takes me sky high.

When we come up for air, he says, "I hate to leave Paris, but Rome awaits us."

"I can't wait."

"And then there's just one more thing we need to do to make the summer complete."

I screw up my face a little at his forwardness and assumption. "Look, Patrick, I'm not ready to go all the way, yet."

He laughs really hard at me. "God, Kendall. Get your mind out of the gutter. I'm not talking about sex." Then he grows serious. "No… we're going to complete the journey and get you your answers."

"Where are we going?"

"*Strada Provinciale 42,*" he whispers.

EPILOGUE

O liver pulled off the biggest coup of all time. Even bigger that the three a.m. elevator ride to the top of the Eiffel Tower.

In Rome, Patrick, Jayne, and I conduct a gallery reading to a standing room only crowd on the rooftop deck of the Hotel Colosseum, followed by a ghost hunt at the Coliseum where the gladiators used to battle. Holy cow...what an experience! Let's just say, we got EVPs from a couple of emperors, the cries of some tortured victims, and even the roar of a lion. I had to beg off the long, pleading story of one gladiator spirit who wanted to tell me all of his experiences. Perhaps another time.

I have a train to catch.

"Hurry up, you two," my aunt says.

I give Jayne my e-mail and promise to stay in touch.

I hug Celia, Taylor, and, yes, even Jason. He and I are just fine.

"Good luck," Celia says to me. "I hope you find what you're looking for."

I squeeze her hand and glance over at Patrick. "I already have." Then my eyes shift to Jason. "As have you."

She blushes, which is ridonkulously endearing. "Enjoy Naples! See you back in Radisson."

"Kendall! Now!" Andi screams out.

We make it to the train station and board our Eurostar headed north from Rome up toward the Switzerland border to seek out the villa from my dreams and visions. This time, Patrick and I share a compartment and I sleep soundly in his arms while we chug along overnight for about seven hours to our destination.

Aunt Andi secures a white Renault Megane Cabrio convertible rental car—that Patrick has to drive because it's a stick shift and my aunt doesn't know how to drive it—and we head off in search of the address from my vision in the luxurious Italian village on the edge of Lake Como.

"This is it," I say, completely recognizing the soft yellow villa with the red roof top. "*Strada Provinciale 42*."

I sit in the passenger seat, frozen to the leather.

"Well?" Patrick asks.

I gulp down the lump of trepidation that's formed in my throat. "Umm…"

Aunt Andi rubs my shoulders from behind. "It'll be fine. You've come this far."

"Yeah, but can I take those last few steps?"

Patrick takes my hand. "I'll be right there with you."

Carefully, I open the car door and step out. With one foot slowly landing in front of the other, I walk up the cobblestone path. Patrick follows two steps behind me. The front door to the villa is open.

"Hello?"

No answer.

"Try it in Italian," Patrick suggests.

"Right." I think for a second to what the guy at the rental car company had said. I've got it. "*Buon giorno!*"

Still nothing.

Patrick shoos me ahead with the wave of his hands.

Instead of walking through the house—which even though I've done it in my dream, it would be presumptuous and rude to actually do it now—I peel off to the right and follow the garden path around the house. Rosemary bushes sing out their woodsy scent, mixing with thyme, basil, and juniper all growing nearby. I pick a twig of sage from the next plant and twirl the soft leaf in my fingers. It reminds me of Thanksgiving and family.

A family that has infinitely extended for me recently.

And now, I take another step.

"You can do it, babe," Patrick encourages.

I round the corner of the house and am aghast that the actual scenery perfectly matches that of my dream. I'm on a deck or balcony that overlooks the majestic, blue mountains and calm, glassy lake. Sitting at the outdoor glass table is an older woman in a light blue maxi dress. She's sipping a coffee and dallying with a pen that's she's using to fill out a crossword puzzle. Her hair is short and so gray it's almost white. She stopped trying to color it seven years ago and just accepted the color.

For a moment, I stand there quietly and study her. The angle of her nose. The slope of her cheek. The point of her chin. It's familiar to me.

I laugh softly at the knowledge and this seems to get her attention.

She turns and slowly stands up. Our eyes meet up and sync in a harmonious moment where words need not be spoken. I'm psychic after all and, who knows, maybe it was passed down to me from my mother's side of the family. When the woman's crossword puzzle book falls to the wooden floor and she nearly knocks over the table, I know that she...knows.

I swallow hard again, trying to find my voice and get past this silly knot in my throat.

"They said you lived in Wisconsin. At least, that's where I saw you in my first visions."

The woman doesn't blink. "We lived in the north woods of Wisconsin for years. Got tired of the winters."

"I was then shown that you were here in Italy. I had to find you," I say. Looking about, I'm absolutely flabbergasted. I've had psychic visions and predictions before, but never something this crisp, this clear, this... real. "This place is exactly as I pictured it. You're just as I pictured you."

Anna Wynn Faulkner smiles at me. "You look just like her. My Emily."

Ahh...she knows.

Just then, an elderly man steps out onto the balcony and drops his coffee cup. The hot, black liquid spills out in dark puddle at his feet. "Sweet Jesus! Emily?"

"John! Look at that mess you've made," Anna says.

He looks to his wife. "It can't be."

I take a deep breath. "No, sir, I'm Kendall."

Anna steps forward and takes my hand. "This isn't Emily, John. But it's her daughter. Our granddaughter."

I smile broadly. "Yes, ma'am. I'm Emily's daughter. You're my grandparents. I dreamed about you."

She puts her hand on my face, trembling, but lovingly warm and soft.

"I dreamed about you, too. Many times." Then she begins to cry. "Many, many times."

Then I'm enveloped in tender embraces from all around me that do not question, doubt, or quibble.

Pure acceptance.

And love.

Definitely love.

Suddenly, I'm home.

Excerpt from *Poser*

Prologue

I'm Chai Devareaux. Yeah, like the tea, thanks. Never heard that reference before. What can I say, my mom went through an existential stage during her pregnancy with me when she left New York and lived in Tibet for several months with (not with-with) the Dali Lama. I suppose my name could be worse.

By day, I'm your average seventeen year old senior at Miami's South Beach High who hangs out with my friends, enjoys the beach (when I have time in my schedule) and works to keep up my grades so Columbia University will admit me to their pre-med program (it's not an official pre-med program, but I'm kind of doing a create your own platter sort of thing) in the fall.

But the minute the last school bell rings—and into the wee hours of the night—I transform. I become the girl in front of the camera with the smoky eyes, perfectly styled hair, and fitted designer clothes. (Okay, so they have to photograph me at the right angle to make sure my not-so-perfect nose looks straight.)

It's all an act, though. A façade for the tabloid rags and entertainment shows that want dirt on my mother and me. (She loves the press!)

You've seen me. I'm the girl in all the hottest clubs where the beautiful people frequent and the fashion photographers gather. I'm never forced to wait at the velvet rope to get inside. I smile (or pout) appropriately when a lens is pointed my way. I strike a pose and show off my Cavalli, my Versace, or my Stella McCartney.

I'm aspiring model...Chai, daughter of 80s fashion icon and former runway diva, Claire-Ann Devareaux...and all that implies.

Not that modeling is what I want to do...but I can't buck Claire-Ann.

I'll admit that I've partied with the Kardashians at The Delano Hotel. I've seen Robert Pattison and Kristen Stewart dancing in darkened corners of the best clubs. I've had dinner with Miley at B.E.D. I've yachted on Biscayne Bay with Beyonce and Jay Z. I have Lindsay Lohan's e-mail address, not that I want to be seen with her anymore.

You might think I live the quintessential life. You might be jealous of the parties I go to and the stars I rub elbows with. Big freaking deal...it's great to have a celebrity for a mother, right? Not when I have to undress her when she's had too much to drink, or hide my face in class at school when my friends see her photographed with some young stallion, or guest starring on a reality TV show as the blast from the past where people say, "I didn't know Claire-Ann Devareaux was still alive!"

Yeah, Claire-Ann's kind of the Keith Richards of the modeling world...only prettier. An icon in the early 80s, she partied with Janice Dickinson, she did cocaine—God knows what else—with Gia Carangi, and she strutted down the catwalk next to Cheryl Tiegs, Christie Brinkley, and Kathy Ireland. Claire-Ann Devareaux was a star...and still loves the limelight.

And it makes my life a living hell.

Can't I just have a normal mother who makes dinners from the five essential food groups instead of ordering take out or making late night reservations? What about a normal teenagehood where I stay home and watch illegally downloaded torrents of classic old teen angst series like, *Buffy the Vampire Slayer, The OC*, and *Gilmore Girls* instead of frequenting Miami Beach's clubs de jour? Normal seventeen year old behavior instead of pretending to be twenty-two and a sex goddess? I'm still a virgin for Christ's sake!

I want to go off to college, be studious, make my way in life, and become a doctor. Not just any doctor, but a cosmetic surgeon. A good one. A serious one. Not like the ones you see all the time in exposés on whatever cable channel that has nothing better to run at

one o'clock in the morning. You know, those doctors who special-
ize in breast enhancement and collagen lips for anyone who walks
in the door. I'll never mutilate beautiful women like my mother
who insist on eternal youth and beauty with face lifts, chemical
peels, and Botox instead of aging gracefully.

No, instead, I'll treat burn victims, cancer patients, and people
disfigured at birth. I'll make sure that everyone's true beauty can
shine through.

That is, if Columbia accepts me.

Don't tell Claire-Ann I applied... she's liable to freak out.

It's hard concentrating on school and my studies since Claire-
Ann has to turn me into a clone of herself. Clubs, private parties,
photo shoots, go-sees, late dinners, champagne toasts, and men,
men, men. Pawing at me and wanting a piece of me all because of
who my mother is...who she was.

Just wait... when I turn eighteen, I'll be free and can be on my
own to do what I want. I'm totally moving to New York.

Yeah, I might look like I have it made. However, I'm anything
but happy.

I'm such a poser.

CHAPTER ONE

"Chai! Come on, Squirt. We've got to get going, the car's waiting," Claire-Ann shouts up the stairs of our massive penthouse loft that overlooks South Beach and the Atlantic Ocean.

I cringe and keep brushing the knot out of my dark brown hair. Hair that's way too long for its own good. Claire-Ann won't dare let me cut it; no way, no how.

"Why does she always call you 'Squirt?'" my best friend, Katy Kingston, asks from my bed. She's sprawled out painting her nails with my Club Monaco Nail Lacquer Duo of Froth and Wave. I picked it up at the photo shoot yesterday afternoon for Fendi Casa Designs, a local Miami Beach furniture designer. I was lying on this sand-colored satin couch with my hand draped over my face. To hide my slightly crooked schnoz, no doubt.

I reach for my bottle of perfume and spritz a stream on my neck and chest. To hell with that crap about spray, delay, and walk away. If I pay good money for this stuff, it's going *on* me. It's this thing I have for smells. Or rather, my fear that *I'll* smell. Shower time prior to an evening out is a ritual in itself for me. Deodorant soap followed by a luffaing with body scrub. Then there's the whole lather, rinse, repeat, condition with a cleansing shampoo and deep conditioner I buy religiously. Once I'm out of the shower, it's time for clear gel stick deodorant, followed by a good blast of deodorant spray, a generous spread of shea butter lotion and foot relief. I also overdo it on the facial moisturization so as to not have to resort to face lifts when I'm in my late forties (like my mother.) First, a layer of skin texture lotion, followed by some moisture surge and a good dabbling around the eyes with some de-aging cream.

But back to Katy's question instead of cataloging the products spread out before me. "Claire-Ann calls me 'Squirt' in reference to my conception."

"Huh?"

"Frozen Pop. Sperm donor. Get it. Squirt."

"Ohhhh, that's right! I keep forgetting that. Shit, Chai, don't you ever wonder who the guy was?"

I shrug as I reach for my lipstick. It's always been Claire-Ann and me... no one else. "You can't miss what you've never had, you know? I mean, I know he was a student in New York back in the late 80s and was supposedly becoming a doctor. That's all I really need to know."

Maybe that's why I have this internal itch to go into the medical profession myself. Seems like the Frozen Pop passed on his learning genes. God knows, I certainly didn't get my academic achievement from high school drop-out, Claire-Ann.

Katy blows on her wet nails and leans back on my bed. "See, if it were me, I'd have to, like, call the Sperm Bank of New York and find out who the swimmers belonged to. What my roots and heritage are."

"Roots and heritage? Are you Alex Haley? You should be in drama club instead of me," I say with a laugh. "It's pretty simple. Claire-Ann had reached a point in her life where she wanted off the drugs and wanted a baby. She bought a test tube and *voila*, Instant Chai."

"You're so blasé about it."

"Why shouldn't I be? It's not like I can change it."

"It's just so...weird, Chai."

"It's never been an issue, honestly."

Katy tosses her short, bobbed blonde hair around. "I couldn't go through life not knowing who my dad is."

I drop the silver lipstick case onto the table. "That's 'cause your dad is one of the richest men in Miami."

This time it's Katy's turn to shrug. Kathryn Irene Kingston lives the perfect life, ensconced in her Star Island mansion (next door to Ja Rule—actually, he's just renting, but still...), her mom works for the Miami Beach Tourism Bureau and her rich father lavishes them with expensive gifts galore. Not that I want that, but her mom cooks a mean pot roast, helps Katy with her homework, and encourages her to go to college instead of pushing her toward the cutthroat world of fashion modeling.

"Chai, are you ready?" Claire-Ann shouts again. Only this time, I hear her coming up the stairs.

"I'm almost done."

"Wear the gold sandals I bought you last week. They'll make your legs look a mile long. You need to be taller."

Right, because models have to be a certain weight and height. Heaven forbid that my five-eight isn't considered Glamazon enough. I'm sure that's my father's fault.

Claire-Ann enters my bedroom decked out in hip BCBG fashion (that's probably too young-looking for her, but she wears it well) and her makeup draw perfectly on her too-too tightly pulled face. Damn Dr. Sheldon for the last face lift that makes her appear slightly Asian.

"Hey, Katy. You going with us, honey?" Claire-Ann asks.

"Not tonight. I have a date with Rick Sommers."

"On a Thursday night?" I ask, like it's some big deal for anyone in our clique to go out on a school night. God knows Claire-Ann drags me out enough when I should be doing homework.

"It's a study date," Katy says, beaming. She's been digging Rick for a time now. Good for her making some headway with him.

I sigh. Katy gets to do real high school things, like study and go on dates—with one of the hottest hunks in school—and go to bed at a decent hour. Me, I'm up all night, in the gym first thing in the morning, and then I hit the ground running with school, photo shoots, and just being Claire-Ann's daughter, which is a full-time job in itself. It's amazing I can keep up this pace she's got me on without major medication. Besides, the guys at school who've shown interest in me only pay attention to me because of my quasi-celebrity status. High school boys are so stupid. I can't wait to get to college.

"Rick's the guy Chai says you've got the hots for?" Claire-Ann prods.

"Mom!" She hates when I address her that way.

She hands me a glass of champagne. "Well, that's what you told me. Remember to use a condom, Katy."

Katy rolls her eyes and laughs. She thinks Claire-Ann is the coolest and that I'm totally lucky to have a mom like her. Me, I want a real mom, not a girlfriend.

Claire-Ann waggles the crystal flute at me. "Here, have some before we leave. This is a big night."

Big indeed. It's Betty Ford Night at Reprise, a hot club attached to Eden's Garden down below Fifth Street that allows eighteen plus in on week nights. I tamp down my disgust at poking fun of the long ago-former first lady's penchant for alcohol. Hell, I don't even get carded there, or anywhere for that matter. Age has never been an issue for me. I look older than my years and when I'm with Claire-Ann, no one questions.

At Reprise, you can usually spot a good portion of the Miami Dolphins' defensive core puffing away on cigars and pounding back expensive cocktails, as well as various Heat players and Marlins hitters, not to mention the hottest people in the hip-hop music scene. Miami Beach is da bomb, da place. And Reprise is a see-and-be-seen sort of establishment. No cutoff jeans and tourist shirts there.

Tonight, Claire-Ann is in search of producers to pitch her new reality TV show idea, as well as a photographer who'll make me his protégée. Both ideas are like looking for the proverbial needle in the haystack. I just want to take a long, hot bath and read the latest David Baldacci novel Katy brought me.

"I don't want champagne," I say, picking up the convo with my mom. Champagne again. Always champagne with Claire-Ann. The stuff gives me a headache. Unlike other people my age who would be super-psyched at being supplied booze by their parents. To me it's no big deal when it's handed to you. Where's the challenge? How is that rebelling?

For me, rebellion comes in the form of an online Common Application aimed at Columbia University's Admissions Office.

But we won't tell Claire-Ann about that *just* yet.

It's not that I hate my mother. I don't. At all. I love her and she's a great person. Thing is, she wants me to be *her*. She'd give nothing more than for me to be a top fashion model at eighteen—just like she was. Of course, Claire-Ann was escaping an abusive, dysfunctional family in Ohio when she broke free and got discovered in New York in the late 70s. She had that feathered, fashionable-then hair that would've made Farrah Fawcett look like a hag. I mean, I give the modeling my all—for Claire-Ann's sake—and I try to succeed, but in the past year since I started this whole "Chai needs to be a model" thing, I seem to only get jobs that her friends hire for or ones that feature poses that hide my—

"Put a little more base and powder on the top of your nose, sweetie, to de-emphasize that crook." Claire-Ann leans in and reaches for the large makeup brush. "Let me."

Hastily, I shove her away and bite on my bottom lip. Yes, okay, I have a bit of a crooked nose! I know it, Katy knows it, everyone at school knows it, Claire-Ann knows it, and so do most of the photographers in the Miami area. It's not like I'm disfigured, though. Enough with the exaggeration and dramatics. God knows I've had to learn to pose properly to make sure it doesn't take over the photos.

I mean, look at Owen Wilson. He's a total babe who gets plenty of movie deals and his nose looks like it survived a car wreck or a crack with a baseball bat. Why is my nose a constant topic of conversation?

Claire-Ann even took me in—I thought we were going in for one of *her* checkups—to Dr. Sheldon for a consultation for rhinoplasty. I'm sorry, but this is the nose I was born with and it's not *that* bad! Cameron Diaz's nose is a little crooked, too, but it never kept her from getting movie roles. It's part of her charm. Just like Tyra Banks and her big-ass forehead that's made her millions. Besides, I'm certainly not spending weeks with black eyes and bandages and wicked pain just so my nose won't stand out so much. That's so not me.

Nevertheless, I smear the foundation on my nose and blend with a sponge as I stare at myself in the mirror. Actually, I've never thought being a model was my calling in life. I don't consider myself as particularly pretty or traffic stopping, like my mother. Even after five plastic surgeries, she's still head-turningly gorgeous.

When I was little, I successfully eluded many of her attempts to enter me into beauty pageants and modeling competitions. But when I hit sixteen and my boobs fully developed and my waist started curving in just right, Claire-Ann was determined I follow in her footsteps.

My eyes shift up now and I meet her ice blue stare. Not ice blue meaning she's pissed at me. Ice blue in that her eyes are the color of the Arctic waters—her true trademark and the one thing that made her stand out in the fashion crowds of the 80s. Hypnotic. Mesmerizing. Million-dollar orbs.

"That's much better," she says, smiling at me in the reflection. "You sure as shit didn't get that nose from me."

No, I didn't. I didn't get a whole hell of a lot from Claire-Ann except my figure. My dark eyes, dark hair and yes, the nose that offends all came from the Frozen Pop. All right, the nose isn't *that* bad, but with Claire-Ann always pointing it out to me my whole life, I feel like it must look like Gerard Depardieu or something to her. Hmmm...maybe *he* was the sperm donor?

"So who are you guys hoping to meet tonight?" Katy asks. "Big date with Craig, Claire-Ann?"

"No, Craig's nothing serious." Claire-Ann flips her dark blonde hair over her shoulder and examines her makeup in the mirror. "But I did get wind that a couple of producers and some big name photographers will be there this evening."

I sigh extra hard. Craig, a.k.a. Guy of the Moment. He's an investment banker in Miami who has been wooing my mother. I think she's just into him for the sex. And it's me who has to hear them when they're going at it. Ewww! The building's built to withstand hurricane-force winds, but not Claire-Ann's ecstatic shrieks.

"What kind of producers?" Katy asks. She digs conversing with my mother. To her it's like watching *The View* in person.

"Well, my sources tell me there's a guy from Bravo who's scouting for his next big reality show. And since Miami Beach is such a hot locale, what better place to look than here?"

"Why would we care about a reality TV producer?" I ask.

With great excitement, Claire-Ann says, "So we can get our own show! Mother and daughter in the modeling industry. If they can make stars out of a bunch of Orange County housewives and trashy people from the Jersey Shore, why not us? It'll be fabulous."

"Absolutely not! I'm not going to be fodder for people's entertainment pleasure. Jesus, Claire-Ann, it's bad enough you send me on these shoots and stuff without—" I stop myself before I tell her what I really feel like doing this whole modeling thing. The pained look on her face—which is a miracle, considering all of the Botox—says I've almost crossed the line. "I only mean that it's, like, been done before."

Her left brow lifts. "Who?"

"I don't know, but surely it's been done."

She waves me off. "We'll be better than anything that's been on before."

Poor Claire-Ann. The camera doesn't love her like it once did, but she still has feelings for it. Unrequited love.

I stand and smooth out the Prada pants I borrowed from Claire-Ann. I've got them paired with a matching designer top that has a square neckline with a seamed Empire waist. The creamy ivory fabric looks great on my freshly spray-tanned skin. It may be early March in South Beach, but I've had nada time to get any sun with the schedule I've been keeping. It's all I can do to keep up my grades, hoping Columbia University will deem me suitable for entrance into their freshman class in the fall.

Claire-Ann strokes my long hair and smiles approvingly. "There's my lovely girl. I'll meet you downstairs. Katy, we can drop you off on the way if you want."

"That's okay, Claire-Ann. I've got my car," Katy says. She hops off the bed and hands over the *Vogue* magazine that's been sitting beside her. "Too bad you have to go to this party and can't stay home gawking at your boyfriend."

"My boyfriend? What the—"

I look at the magazine and nearly gasp when I see the photo she's pointing out. Ooo, hadn't seen that yet. Droolingly handsome, barefoot Ty Willingham dressed in white linen Armani suit in a two-page spread. The guy's got piercing chocolate eyes, a stern chin with his signature cleft in it, and thick, shiny black hair. My fingers could get lost in that mop for at least a week. No one on earth should be allowed to look that fucking amazing.

Except maybe male super model extraordinaire, Ty Willingham. I can't believe this guy is my age.

"God, I wish he *were* my boyfriend," I say with a bit of a sigh. "I wouldn't have to think twice about giving him my virginity."

Katy lights up. "You know, I read on the InsaneMiami blog that he and his family are moving here. His father is this power stock broker in Manhattan who had a heart attack, so the doctors told him to move to a warmer climate."

My heart trips over itself at the thought of running into Ty Willingham on Ocean Drive or at one of the hotel bars on Collins. Of meeting him and sharing a moment. Of falling at his feet and admitting that I have a poster of him on the inside of my closet door. So juvenile of me, but a girl can dream.

"Chai Devareaux!" Claire-Ann calls out from the lower level. "Get your skinny little ass down here now! Our car service is waiting!"

"Wish me luck tonight," I say to Katy as I grab my sparkly clutch. "Claire-Ann's convinced, as you saw, that tonight's the night I get discovered."

Katy screws up her face. "But is that what you want?"

I let out a long breath. "It's what Claire-Ann wants. And as long as I'm under her roof, living off her money and all that stuff, I've got to do as she says. Besides, I'm not in drama class for nothing. I can act exactly like she wants: mature, sophisticated, fashionable, and most of all, interested."

"Okay, strut your stuff, g'friend. If there's one thing you *did* inherit from her, it's your walk. Go get 'em, babe!"

Heading down the stairs, I stand tall and confident, ready to face the long evening ahead. Underneath the foofed hair and perfect makeup is the real me. The girl who simply wants to go to college, get away from her mom, be on her own. The woman beneath the façade who longs to be a doctor, help others, and make a difference.

For tonight—and for the next few weeks (until I hear from Columbia) I'll suck it up and keep playing the game. I've done so well up until now.

At the base of the staircase, Claire-Ann puts her hand over her heart. "You truly are breathtaking, sweetie."

And somehow, I feel like I am.

ACKNOWLEDGMENTS

First and foremost, huge thanks to my awesome agent, Deidre Knight, for helping me keep this series going. To Jia Gayles, for all of her amazing assistance in the process.

To my critique partner, Wendy Toliver, for keeping me focused, for reading for me, and for being an all-around fabulous person. I'm in awe of you. Truly.

To Google…what would I do without you?

To my fan and friend, Jayne Mcburney, who let me borrow her name for a character in this story. Hope I did you proud.

To all the fans who patiently waited over a year for the continuation of this story. I can't thank you enough for your support and for loving Kendall and company as much as I do. If you'd like to see more adventures, please e-mail me at marley.h.gibson@gmail.com and let me know!

And to my wonderful husband, Patrick Burns, not only for his love and continuing support, but for driving extra shifts during our travels to afford me more writing time. You're the best and I'm so glad I'm on this journey with you.

ABOUT THE AUTHOR

Marley Gibson is a young adult, contemporary romance, and non-fiction author best known for her wildly popular GHOST HUNTRESS series. Gibson appeared on the premiere episode of Biography's "My Ghost Story," as well as being on episodes of the Travel Channel's "Paranormal Challenge," and "Ghost Adventures." A certified SCUBA diver, a closet gourmet chef, and an avid traveler, Marley lives in the Florida Keys with her husband, Patrick Burns from TruTV's "Haunting Evidence," and their two rescue kitties, Madison and Boo. When she's not crafting novels, she makes hand-crafted zombie baby dolls called DagNabIt Dolls that are all the rage! She can be found online at www.marleygibson.com, Facebook at marley.h.gibson, and Twitter @MarleyGibson. DagNabIt Dolls can be found on Facebook at www.facebook.com/DagNabItDolls/ or at www.dagnabitdolls.com.

CPSIA information can be obtained at www.ICGtesting.com
Printed in the USA
LVOW10s1738210715

447055LV00007B/1085/P